Socially Awkward

STEPHANIE HADDAD

Cover design by Emily S. Rubenstein

Copyright © 2012 Stephanie Haddad

All rights reserved.

ISBN: 1466452781
ISBN-13: 978-1466452787

For SMC, SPC, & SLC

Sisters are friends forever.

PROLOGUE

My name is Olivia Saunders, but my friends just call me Livy. If you happen to stumble upon my Facebook profile, you'll learn pretty much all there is to know about me. As the daughter of a US Army sergeant, I spent my early years moving all around the world in an exciting blur of activity, new faces, and strange places. I'm an only child, a daddy's girl, and yet I have no desire to join the military whatsoever. And yes, people ask me that question all the time.

Growing up, I followed my dad and mom from Boston to London, Texas, New York, and even Germany. Thanks to all of the moving around, I've acquired a diverse range of skills, which include hunting for quail, repairing a riding lawn mower, and hosting a proper tea time with real English scones I can bake from scratch. I speak three languages fluently, have extensive training in horseback riding, and almost made the Olympic women's volleyball team just after I graduated high school. My interests are as varied as the places I've lived and I always love to try new things, whether it's knitting or base jumping.

Looking back on my life, now that I'm an adult, I've seen so many places and met so many people that it sometimes seems there's nothing left to explore. My one regret, however, is never growing any real roots anywhere. It's the one experience I've never had: to find somewhere I belong and learn to fit in.

That is, until I moved back to Boston a few years ago to pursue a career in modeling. I know, most people think of New York or Paris as the only runways worth walking. Having been to both cities, I knew neither was the right scene for me. I gave up on my dream of turning on the big catwalks of the world in favor of a calmer, quieter modeling career concentrated on print advertisements and catalogs. Take a look at my profile photos and think really hard about where you've seen me. You'll probably have some distant memory of seeing me somewhere before.

Now that I've finally found someplace to call my home city, I'm hoping to settle down. Unfortunately, my modeling contacts aren't exactly great marriage material, especially since most of the men I know are playing for the other team. That's why I've turned to social networking to meet new people, both close to home and overseas, wherever the web takes me. I've made hundreds of virtual new acquaintances, some with similar interests and some with very different ways of looking at the world. Yet they're all my friends, some with the potential to become more. Maybe one of them is the lucky one I've been waiting for.

Currently, that list of friends is more than 800 strong—an impressive feat considering I have never actually met a single one of them in person. Some of them might try to argue that they *do* know me from their days at school or perhaps met me at that one party that time at that girl's house. Maybe they think they recognize me from last fall's catalog, or that billboard ad they drive past every day.

But they'd all be wrong, because Olivia Saunders doesn't exist.

In real life, my name is Jennifer Smith, and I, like my name, am almost the perfect picture of normalcy. In fact, I'm still a little angry with my parents for giving me the Number One most common name for girls during the year I was born. Paired with the Number One most common surname in the United States, I'm as boring and invisible as a name can make a person. I'm the very image of the "girl next door," American as apple pie. With smooth skin, plain features, and a little too much weight around my middle, I look like almost every other girl I've ever met. Except for two tiny details: a pair of "accessories" I wish I didn't need but cannot live without.

I guess that's where this idea of Olivia Saunders came from. She's exotic and special in every way I'm not. She's unique and distinctive in the right ways... rather than because she wears hearing aids as a result of a birth defect to her hearing nerves. Not like the real me.

CHAPTER ONE

"How could you do this to me?" Gaping at my sister, the very person I've called my best friend for basically my entire life, these are the only words I can muster.

Claire stands still, staring back at me, but doesn't say a word in her own defense. She just freezes, hands on her slender hips, and focuses her blue eyes like laser beams at my skull. As her anger bubbles under the surface of her expression, I can see her little button nose twitching with frustration.

"I trusted you and now..."

Her eyes grow big at my words, her anger spilling over the edge. "It's this stupid project, Jen! It's taking over your entire life! You don't see things right anymore. You don't get it, do you? Sean doesn't love *you*, he's in love with *Olivia*. It seems hardly fair that you're mad at me about this."

"But I *am* Olivia, Claire!" I blink, biting back tears. I never thought, in all the years of being the victim of bully after bully, that my own sister could hurt me the deepest. Never.

"No, you're not. There is no Olivia! I just don't see what the problem is. He cares about me now," she offers, hands on her hips. Her tone softens, but her words don't cut me any less deeply. "And I care about him. Can't you just be happy for us?"

It's all my fault, of course. Or rather, Olivia's fault. If only I'd just picked something else to study for my sociology project, things could have been so different. Now it's far too late. The damage has been done.

"You know damn well what you're doing and how wrong it is!" I don't want to yell, but I'm starting to lose both the feeling in my face and all of my vocal control. "You're stealing Sean because I showed you what kind of person Tom really is! It's not my fault what he did to you, Claire."

"This has nothing to do with that," Claire says, her tone growing icy.

"I said I was sorry, Claire. I had no idea he would…"

"Why can't you just mind your own business, Jen? Just go be with Noah and leave me the hell out of it!"

It's my turn to turn icy, as my eyes narrow on my spiteful sister. "Leave Noah out of this, Claire. You know damn well there's nothing going on between…"

"For the love of God, Jen! You just want them all for yourself, don't you?"

"I'm not the one of us who's a selfish bitch!"

As soon as the words explode from my mouth, I want to stuff them back in. Claire is not a bitch, she never has been. But I just don't have a word to describe what she's become in these past few weeks. There's a pause between us, a mutual look of shock that divides us like steel bars down the center of the room. To cover up my embarrassment, I yell even louder. "Just get out!"

"Girls!" When my mother bursts through the side door, Claire and I freeze.

We often forget how thin the walls are between my parents' house and the in-law apartment I live in. It's just one of the pitfalls of living here, being so exposed all the time. I enjoy the part with low rent and no utilities, the built-in laundry service, and the access to home-cooked meals when I want them, but it's annoying to have unannounced family visits at any time of the day.

"Great job, Jen. Now the authorities are involved," Claire's sarcasm falls flat in the silent apartment. My mother stares us down, each in turn, until Claire throws her hands up into the air. "Forget it. I'm out of here."

Mom and I watch Claire storm out the front door, leaving it open, without even putting her jacket on. The weather has been warming up lately, but the cold spring air blows briskly into my apartment. Still, what really gives me chills is the memory of Claire's expression when I mentioned Tom.

What the hell have I done?

Eventually, Mom coaxes me onto the sofa with a cup of tea, wraps a blanket around my shoulders to protect against the chill, and sits down next to me. She gives me a speech about how she's still our mother, even though her babies are all grown up now, and that we can come to her about anything, anytime. These are all facts I've known all along, but confessing to my mother, of all people, the horrible things I've done just makes me feel even more despicable.

"I... can't, Mom," I manage to say, stirring the spoon in my tea unconsciously. We stare at each other in silence for several moments. Her thin lips pull into a tight line as she observes my expression, distorted with emotional turmoil, and the corners shift downward into a frown. "It's a really long story and I..."

"Jennifer," she says, narrowing her eyes—her eyes that are just like Claire's, only much wiser. And far less judgmental. "Do you have someplace better to be? Because your father fell asleep an hour ago watching golf and I've got a free evening to occupy. Humor me."

I chuckle, despite myself, and try to steel my nerves. "If I tell you, just promise you won't think any less of me... okay? I didn't mean for any of this to happen. It's all gotten out of hand and I'm... I don't know what to do."

Mom leans in and kisses my forehead, smoothing a strand of hair behind my hearing aid. It jostles a bit but doesn't come out of place. I take a deep breath and begin.

To effectively tell my story, I should start a little closer to the beginning. Before Sean, Tom, Noah, and even Olivia came into our lives. Before Claire and I ever fought about anything more serious than who got the bigger scoop of ice cream. Before my mother was a frequent interrupter of key conflicts in my apartment. Before I'd ever created that fake Facebook profile.

This whole mess started as a fleeting thought, inspired by a discussion in one of my graduate classes. And now it's threatening to destroy everything I love… just like Frankenstein's monster. Why, oh why, didn't I just get my degree in Literature?

All I needed was an idea for my final paper for my Master of Science in Sociology. Since it was already September of my final year in the program, I was a bit desperate. I wasn't in one of those Master's programs where you just read a bunch of books, repackaged some ideas, and made it sound pretty in about 50 pages. Oh no. Instead, I was required to conduct actual field research.

But I'll admit it: I was completely devoid of ideas. Except for those offered by my sister Claire, which were completely horrible: "Study freshmen at the laundromat and write about how clueless kids are away from their mommies the first time" or, my favorite, "Study the social interactions between police officers and people getting speeding tickets." In hindsight, either one of those might have been a more practical choice of research project. Even her idea about the social interactions of gardeners and their plants was better than this.

Bad idea after bad idea, Dr. Chase, my advisor and the professor of my Contemporary Issues in Sociology course, just kept telling me not to panic. In part, I blame her for not putting the kibosh on this thing right away. If she had just assigned me a topic, maybe I wouldn't have jumped on the first "decent" idea I came across. Maybe.

I start my story for Mom on the day this mess really began. The planets were all aligned and the moon was full… or something. But still, I was late for my morning lecture.

Dr. Chase was already talking at rapid pace when I slid into the back of the small room and joined the rest of the class. It was one of my last course requirements, with just two semesters left to create the perfect research study.

My professor glanced up from her lecture notes on the podium and nodded at me. A few students swiveled in their chairs to see who had just cut into the middle of their class, but most of them probably assumed it was me and didn't even flinch. Two weeks into the semester, they should all be used to my tardiness by now. Call it bad luck or just poor planning, but something always delayed me.

"You'll be late for your own funeral, Jen," my mother chuckles, interrupting my story. I groan and continue.

I took my usual seat in the back, pulled out my trusty iPad and started jotting some notes. Dr. Chase was talking about the relationships between friends and how they have been altered in our present day, thanks to advances in technology. Advances like the one I was definitely not using to surf the web in the middle of her class time. Still... if I was Googling "modern sociology" for a research project topic, was that really a waste of said class time?

"How do you communicate with your closest friends today?" she asked the class, breaking the fast clip of her own lecture. "Has it changed in the past few years? Your generation has experienced a huge shift in the way people keep in touch, so how has that affected your lives?"

I lifted my head to acknowledge that I heard the question but didn't have a response. Dr. Chase looked around the room, eyebrows raised, waiting for the first hands to go up.

"Anyone?" she asked again.

A few people raised their hands, and Chris Tuckerman gave some response about text messaging and how he could instantly get responses from his friends, instead of wasting time with a game of phone tag. This, apparently, made the process of making plans to "hang out" go much more smoothly. Lyla Crosby offered her own response next, diving head-first into a conversation about how much American Online's instant messaging changed American speech. AIM, she claimed, was responsible for the first short form communication with abbreviations like LOL and BRB. I didn't want to embarrass her in front of the class by explaining that secretaries actually used short-hand notations like that for faster dictation over fifty years ago, and just went back to my web browsing.

I could study secretarial sociology, perhaps, I thought, scanning down the list of links presented to me by Google. Ooh! Over socialization—that could be an interesting topic, right? I clicked on the link and waited for the page to load. Take. For. Ever. Why don't you?

I knew I should be listening, but most of the class discussion bounced off of me like tennis balls on a court. It was hard to come up with something meaningful to say when your closest friend in the world was the big sister who used to steal your dessert, listen in on your phone calls (when you got them), and frame you for every broken lamp in the house. I love Claire more than anyone in the world, but seriously, what could I have contributed to that conversation? Technology might have made it easier for Claire to nag me about getting a new inspection sticker for my car, but that was about it. Had it really done anything to alter our relationship?

Let's not even discuss the fact that sisters don't really count as friends. Do they? I thought they were kind of a given. You know, you're born to the same parents, so you almost *have* to have something in common. Or at least a reason to care whether the other one is still breathing or not.

"Jennifer? Anything to add?" said Dr. Chase suddenly.

I froze with my pen hanging out of my mouth, and shifted my irises to the front of the room. Dr. Chase stared at me, looking rather stately behind her wooden podium. I could feel my temperature rising, the blood pooling in my cheeks. All eyes were riveted to my reddening face. I had no idea where the conversation had traveled while I'd been lamenting my poor, lonely existence. And web-surfing, too, but mostly lamenting.

Think, Jen. Think, think!

"Um, I…" Not good enough. Luckily, Dr. Chase saw my struggle, took pity, and decided to throw me a bone.

"Regarding communication via the web?" she said, folding her hands together and watching me patiently.

"Well, I guess it provides us with a certain amount of anonymity," I ventured, giving my professor a cautious look. She nodded, urging me onward. "Sure, we can talk to our friends online, but it also opens up a whole new world of strangers to converse with. People we might never attempt to speak to in real life, like at the grocery store or in a college class."

I tried really hard not to look at the couple of football players sitting together in the front of the class, but my ridiculous, wandering eyes betrayed me. One of them even winked at me, because he's a huge jerk who thinks he's hot enough to rattle a quiet, nerdy girl like myself. I guess some of us haven't actually graduated from high school yet. I shook it off like a champ and looked back at Dr. Chase.

"In essence," I continued. "I suppose we're almost redefining the word *friend* today with certain forms of online communication."

"Meaning?" Dr. Chase leaned forward with her elbows on the podium, smiling. At some point, she'd slid her silver wireframe glasses onto her head. She was definitely into whatever it was I was trying to say. I decided to keep talking, cautious not to sound like a desperate loser with no friends who hangs out on the internet all day.

"Well, I have *lots* of so-called friends on Facebook who are much more like drive-by acquaintances or friends of friends. Some of them are people I once went to school with and never even liked, who wouldn't have given me the time of day if I spontaneously caught on fire during a Calculus class." This earned a few chuckles, so I paused until the room grew quiet again. "In person, I might spot these people across a department store and run the other way. But online, we're the kind of friends who post comments on each other's photos or send Happy Birthday wishes back and forth. I think the internet lets us all be hypocrites."

My classmates remained silent for a moment, as Dr. Chase's eyes scanned the room, looking for reactions. A few of them looked puzzled, with an eyebrow raised or a head tilted to the side, but my professor seemed pleased. As I let my own words sink through my thick skull, I started to realize how unique a viewpoint I might have stumbled upon.

After class, Dr. Chase intercepted me on my way out.

"Well, Jen, I think we've found your topic." She seemed pleased to have inspired me with such a great idea. Or at least to have hosted such a great debate in her classroom for a change.

"Internet hypocrisy?" I asked, skeptically.

Dr. Chase exhaled deeply, giving herself some time to think. "Maybe not as such, but there's something to what you were saying about having a dual personality, on and off the web. I think it might be an interesting study to look at perception and falsehood on the internet. Maybe see what you can discover."

"Do you really think so? I don't even know how to go about doing this." I smoothed my long brown hair on both sides, being sure to cover my hearing aids. Nervous habit.

"Well, it's up to you how to proceed," said Dr. Chase, shoving a stack of notebooks and essay papers into her tote bag. "But I think you need to explore the anonymity and duplicity you were talking about. Find a way to really dig deep into these aspects of social media and I think you've got yourself a paper."

Basically, it was the beginning of the end.

CHAPTER TWO

"So, where does Olivia fit in?" Mom interrupts again.

"I'm getting to that, Mom. See, I spent a few days thinking about the internet hypocrisy thing and kept coming up empty handed. I couldn't find a way to do the research on something like that. It was too big to tackle the regular way."

She nods, taking my empty tea cup and setting it on the coffee table.

"It wasn't until I went to my doctor's appointment later that week that I really came up with something..."

As I took the bus down Commonwealth Ave to my doctor's office, I tried to think about other things. Frustrated, I'd let the idea of my research project go for a little while. I had other things to worry about. My appointment that day was the dreaded annual physical, one that tended to haunt me for the months that followed it. For some reason, my doctor and I were having a constant disagreement about a hot-button topic: my weight. While I felt that it was simply an area that needed improvement, nothing life-threatening, she wouldn't let the subject go.

Granted, my weight was one improvement I'd been "working on" for a long time. When I say I'd been working on it,

I mean that I kept thinking about exercising, but ended up praying instead to wake up one morning in a normal size—like an 8 or a 10, not super skinny or anything. Just healthy.

Even with the extra pounds on my frame, I was still pretty healthy. Healthy enough. I only got sick, like, once a year... and my acne was finally starting to clear up. That was a definite plus; especially since I'd heard a lady at a cosmetics counter once say that healthy skin reflects a healthy inside. Obviously, I had nothing to worry about.

So why did my doctor disagree with me every time I saw her?

"Jennifer," Dr. Brinkley sighed, flipping through the pages of my chart at my annual physical. She is a tall, thin woman with a bird-like nose. Her white blond hair is always impeccable in a neat chignon and the clothing she wears under her lab coat is usually the latest from the Talbot's rack. Not that I would wear anything from Talbot's, at the risk of looking like a somewhat fashionable plain-clothes nun, but I didn't think I would fit into anything in that store anyway.

When Dr. Brinkley cleared her throat, I pulled my eyes away from her crisply creased slacks. Right. I was not here for a fashion consultation.

"Jennifer," she tried again, this time leaning forward over her crossed legs. This was her let's-be-serious-for-a-moment face. I knew it well, given how many times I'd seen it before. "What are we going to do about your situation?"

"Situation?" I adjusted my left hearing aid, pushing it further in. Would she buy it if I played dumb?

"Yes," Dr. Brinkley raised an eyebrow at me, as though challenging me to ask her again. "For the last eight years, we've been talking about the same problem. And for eight years, you've been saying you were going to get healthy."

"But I *am* healthy... enough."

"Sure... Healthy enough for now. But you know very well that this extra weight will put you at risk for some scary things like diabetes and heart disease, among others. I'm not asking you to drop half your body weight here, Jennifer. Even losing ten-percent would significantly reduce your risk factors. If you do nothing, you're just waiting for it to make you sick or, eventually, kill you."

I blinked at her. "Ouch, Dr. Brinkley."

"Well, Jennifer, I'm concerned about you. The time for niceties is over. You need to lose 30 pounds to get yourself to a healthy weight. I can't do it for you." As she said this, Dr. Brinkley reached a hand out to touch my elbow. "Do this for yourself. You deserve to be healthy."

Looking into her eyes, I really wanted to tell her I could do it. That I *would* do it, once and for all. But 30 is such a big, big number... and a bit more than that ten-percent that she was talking about. Where was I supposed to start? "I don't know how to do this... to stay motivated. I keep trying and... then I give up."

"Close your eyes for a minute, Jennifer," she said, her voice more soothing. I looked at her in disbelief. "Just try it, okay?"

I closed my eyes, albeit skeptically, and tried to clear my mind to listen to whatever words of wisdom she was about to impart.

"I want you to picture yourself now, looking into a mirror. See what you see every day and just look for a moment."

I almost winced, visualizing myself reflected in the bathroom mirror. I never liked to look at myself, not any more than necessary. You know, things like checking for misplaced hairs or spinach between my teeth were okay, but that was about it. This time, I tried really hard to see myself and all my imperfections without banishing the image.

"Good," Dr. Brinkley cut in. "Now, imagine what it could be like if you reached your goal. What will you be proud of when you're fitter and leaner? When you've trimmed away the excess and become the you who's inside this person?"

I could see myself transforming. Miraculously, my arms became sculpted, my thighs toned, my middle slimmed away to a healthy size. Somehow, my hair grew longer and turned blonde... but still, I could see that it was still me in the mirror. It was a whole new version of Jennifer and she looked happy.

"Have you got an image of what you'd like to become?"

I nodded, suddenly motivated, and opened my eyes.

"Excellent," she smiled. "The best way to get there is to make small, achievable goals. Break your weight loss down into five pound increments and just move milestone to milestone until you get there. And give yourself a realistic timeline, Jennifer. You can't expect to lose more than a couple of pounds a week at a healthy pace. No crash diets, nothing radical. And I'll be checking in on you during the next few months, okay?"

I kept nodding, feeling like my head might snap off my neck with all the enthusiasm. I knew finally what I had to do, even if it wasn't exactly what Dr. Brinkley had in mind for me.

Twenty minutes later, I left the clinic with much more paperwork than I cared to read. I had pamphlets with titles like *Your Midsection & You*, *15 Bad Eating Habits to Change Today*, and *Yoga for Plus Size Women* just at the top of the pile. There were many more of these things, plus a list of recommendations from Dr. Brinkley. I resisted the urge to pitch everything straight into the trash barrel outside the door and shoved them into my messenger bag instead.

I was walking out of that appointment with much more than boring reading material. Inadvertently, Dr. Brinkley had solved my academic dilemma with her visualization tactics. Losing all that weight still seemed daunting, but becoming the image I'd seen in the mirror was as easy as a Photo Shop edit. I wanted to burst with the excitement of it all. Finally, an idea I could really be passionate about!

Still, it was really tempting to actually take her advice the way it was intended…

As I waited for the bus, I looked down at my midsection and frowned. Why did it have to be so big and frumpy? So squishy and unsightly? Why couldn't I just flatten it with some Spanx every day until it went away? Why did my sister get all the skinny genes, and thus, the skinny jeans? It's just not fair that I had to be Claire's rotund sister, Dr. Brinkley's at-risk patient, my parents' chubby daughter. I just couldn't take it anymore.

Although I hated to admit it to myself, Dr. Brinkley was right. Sighing, I looked up to see the white and yellow T bus approaching. I dug into my pocket for my Charlie Card and paused, my fingers wrapped around the plastic bus pass.

No. No bus today. It's not raining or snowing, and it's actually kind of a nice day. You're walking home, Lazy. Consider this the beginning of your midsection's end.

At home, I sunk into my desk chair and tried to ignore how sweaty I'd gotten from my mere two-mile walk. So, I was out of shape, as it turned out. I didn't need to dwell on this fact; I just needed to change it. So I Googled some workout tips, looked for a few nearby studios that had this plus-size yoga thing Dr. Brinkley was raving about, and settled on a course of action. Then I started tackling the diet part of my weight loss plan, got frustrated at the price of all the delivered-to-your-door meals available out there, and decided I should just close my web browser and eat a Hostess cupcake instead. Yes, that was much easier.

"Stop, stop, stop." I shook my head at myself, and then contemplated getting a cat so it would be a little less weird when I talked to myself at home. Yeah, I'd just be talking to the cat... right.

"Jennifer Smith," I continued. "Step away from the Hostess and get back to work."

By sheer force of my suddenly iron-clad will power, I decided to back out of the kitchen and return to my seat. So the diet plan search was going to be an uphill battle. This was a good thing to be aware of because childhood public service announcements taught me that knowing is half the battle. I couldn't let it throw me off course. I decided to give it a break for tonight and turned, instead, to matters of my education.

Or, rather, my social networking project.

Dr. Brinkley had inspired me with something good, a clear way to demonstrate how the internet allowed people to be hypocritical. And what effect anonymity played on social interactions on the web. If there was a way to do this, and have fun, I was willing to try almost anything.

I closed my eyes, trying to get back that image of the improved version of myself. The beautiful hair, the toned arms, the muscle definition. This new version of me that would exist (maybe someday) in reality, but could also exist (instantly) in the virtual world. But how to get her out there?

It was right about then that Claire burst through my front door, as she has been known to do from time to time. Living a town away seems to offer me very little protection from her sisterly drop-ins.

"Hey Jen," she said, pulling me out of the brain of my imaginary identity. "How's the project coming?"

"How do you do that?" I answered, a bit ruffled.

"What?"

"Always know what I'm thinking about?"

"Duh, I'm your sister." Claire answered, with one hand on her hip. "Also, you're sitting in front of your laptop on a Google search page for 'social anonymity and the internet.' Even John Edwards could read you right now."

I filled her in on my idea in Dr. Chase's class earlier in the week and my inspiration to "pretend" to be someone else. I clicked through a few of the Google search results links while I talked, but couldn't find anything useful to back me.

"It's probably hopeless, though," I sighed, blowing a strand of hair out of my face. "I can't really find any other projects to support it. I don't even know what framework to use for something like this."

"Oh my God, Jen! I've got it!" she said, slapping my shoulder. "You should make a fake Facebook profile! You can be, like, a supermodel or something and try to friend random people. And then, with your real profile, you can try to friend the same people and see how their reactions are different."

I had to give it to Claire. On paper, the premise was perfect. Her endless fountain of ideas, it seemed, had finally turned up a lucky penny. And that's more or less how my final paper, *The Effects of Social Media on Human Interaction*, was born.

"Good title," says my Mom, still paying loyal attention to my rambling story. "Is it finished?"

"We're getting there, Mom," I say patiently, trying to tuck my chilly toes into the fleece blanket. "The problem is, it's a whole lot more than a paper right now. And that was never supposed to happen."

CHAPTER THREE

I didn't waste much time getting started after that. With only a few months left before my deadline, I couldn't afford to spend any more time grueling over the details. So the next day, I dug into the creation of my new fake profile in earnest. I picked a random name that could belong to either someone totally normal or someone crazy famous: Olivia Saunders. I decided that, if I got to play pretend and be someone totally fake, then I might as well go all out. As I typed in my new name, I actually got chills. A whole new me, with full control over every single detail of my life. It was truly exhilarating.

Crafting a whole identity from scratch, I fashioned Olivia as an army brat with a diverse list of random skills, fluent in three languages, and with a career in modeling. To be totally cliché, I also made her an aspiring actress. I listed her current city as Boston, Massachusetts, but the hometown I left blank, due to all of Olivia's family's moves. I checked the box that she was a female and sure, I decided to "show my sex in my profile." Do people really keep that a secret? Why?

I made up a random birthday for my new fake self. But then, given the option, I decided to only show the month and day on my profile, although I have already decided that Olivia is 27, just like me. In her line of work, she might not want people to know she was within throwing distance of age 30. I hardly wanted people to know that, and I don't consider myself half as vain as I would expect someone like Olivia to be.

Next, I clicked that Olivia is interested in men and women. Why not? She might just be that kind of open-minded girl. At the very least, wouldn't it attract a wider range of, ahem, interested parties? For her spoken languages, I entered English, which is a given, as well as Spanish and German. Perfect. I don't speak anything but my native tongue, but I always wished I did. I just hoped no one would try to chat with me in Spanish or German, or I'd be spending a lot of time on Google Translator.

For the time being, I skipped the About Me section, deciding to wait until I had more time to make up something that sounded at least moderately interesting. Maybe Olivia was raised as a circus performer. Was she an award-winning country line dancer? No, too isolating, especially in New England. What if I trained polar bears? The endless possibilities were just too much to handle all at once.

Instead, I kept going, typing in exotic things like "gourmet French cooking" as one of my hobbies and interests. I just typed away until I got to Relationship Status. I thought for a minute, chewing on a hang nail, and decided to keep my options open. Olivia's relationship status would be single. That was one thing the real me and the fake me could agree on.

Profile picture. That was a problem. Okay, so I had lots of pictures of me, but they didn't look like the blonde-haired, green-eyed Olivia Saunders I'd been imagining in my head. I'd have to ask Claire for help fudging this important detail. She would know how to make it look good.

So I called her and told her she had to come over right after work to help me.

I clicked through a few more screens, entered a handful of responses, saved my changes and tada! My new fake profile went live, just like that, ready to be friended by the strangers of the universe. Still, that empty picture box with an androgynous silhouette stared back at me from the screen.

I was eager to see how the virtual world would receive the new, improved me: Olivia Saunders, model and actress. As the other half of the project, I would pit her profile directly against my own real-life one. I made a list of suggested names—men and women who looked fake themselves and a few normal-looking ones here and there—and sent friend requests to them from both Olivia and myself. I typed the names into a spreadsheet, noted the date, and waited to see which boxes I could check. Would one profile appeal over another? Would Olivia's "exotic" and exciting life be perceived as more enticing? Did it matter that these people didn't know either of us at all? With nothing left to do but wait, I started poking around Olivia's profile. I took a few surveys, liked a few supermodels' fan pages, and made a list of some groups she might like to join.

Just as I was getting bored, my sister arrived.

"Hey, Claire!" I greeted her with a hug and an ear-to-ear grin.

She eyed me suspiciously. "So what's this super-important task that only I can help you with?"

I took a deep breath then cracked a wide grin. "Want to Photo Shop me into a hot chick?"

"Come on, Jen. Haven't we talked about the negative effects of your self-deprecating humor enough already?" Claire rolled her eyes, settling in comfortably on my couch.

"Well, if I can't laugh at myself..."

I mean, nobody's perfect. When I looked in the mirror, I could admit that I had a nice smile, pretty eyes, and a generally pleasant appearance. I didn't *hate* myself, but I definitely saw room for improvement. Especially if my hair wasn't covering those hearing aids.

"There's a difference between finding the humor in life and laughing *at* yourself, Jen. Why can't you just use a picture of yourself? What's this *hot chick* nonsense anyway?" Claire reached over to the arm of the couch, seizing my latest issue of *Cosmopolitan* and flipping mindlessly through the pages.

"Well," I began, sitting gingerly into my desk chair. "The whole point of this project is to try to attract people to be my friend. I can't exactly do that when I look like…"

Claire's head rose slowly from the magazine, her gaze locking in on me. "Like *what?*"

"Like this!" I said, gesturing emphatically up and down my body. "Do you really think any guy is going to friend me looking like this? A big, frumpy…"

"Stop it, already. You're not frumpy. There's nothing wrong with you, okay? You're smart, pretty, funny…"

"And overweight, Claire. I'm the fat sister."

She opened her mouth to chide me again, but froze mid-thought. "Hey," she straightened up, leaning forward. "What's that on your shirt?"

I looked down, ready to swat away some giant bug or something, and spotted it. It wasn't alive, nor had it ever been, as far as I could tell. And it should've been in my mouth, not on my shirt.

"It's just a crumb from my lunch, Claire," I shrugged, keeping my eyes carefully averted. As I raised my hand to brush it off, she grabbed my wrist in the air. Wow, she can move fast…

"That looks like chocolate cake. Is that…" Her eyes widened as she held my stare. "Oh, Jen! Is that from a cupcake?"

And just like that, Claire set loose on my kitchen, opening every cabinet and drawer, even checking the fridge. She pulled out a whole bunch of carbo-loaded, fat-laden, tasty morsels that I'd been stockpiling for my last year of grad school. I watched in horror as she tossed them all with wild vengeance into my trash barrel.

"Claire! Stop it!" I held my arms out, not sure what to do, what to rescue from certain doom, or how to stop her. "Leave me alone, Claire!"

She rounded on me, clutching a gigantic bag of gummy bears in two white-knuckled hands. "Do you really need these, Jen? Is it worth it to stuff your face with this, then turn around and make fun of yourself for being overweight?"

Stunned, I let my arms fall to my sides. I knew in my brain that she was right, but I also knew in my heart that I'd eaten that Hostess cupcake—the one whose dirty, shameful crumb had gotten me busted in the first place—without even knowing it. I'd hidden the wrapper in the trash, down below a banana peel and an empty low-fat chip bag, just in case Claire spotted it. All of this I did regularly on autopilot, staring mindlessly at a computer screen or lost in thoughts about a life that wasn't mine.

The truth was, I just didn't know how to be any other way.

"Claire, please. I'm not…" Tears welled in my eyes but I fought to keep them contained.

"I just want to help you," she said, letting the gummy bears fall to the kitchen floor. "I didn't want to upset you. It just hurts me to hear you talk about yourself like that when you could change it, and you don't. Come here."

She held out her arms to me, my beautiful and loving big sister, and I went to her. I hugged her, signaling my forgiveness, and bit down on those tears until they stopped threatening to spill.

"I know, Claire," I said, when I was confident that my voice wouldn't crack. "But I'm not ready to do this. I know it's dumb, but I can't stop it now, Claire. It's too much. Just let me finish with school and maybe I'll be ready then, okay?"

Claire let the topic drop for the time being, leaving the junk food wherever it had landed, strewn about my little galley kitchen. She released me from her embrace and shooed me back into the living room.

Within mere minutes, I had gotten her out of rampage mode and back on track to help me. I knew she only wanted what she believed was best for me, but she should know by now that pushing me does nothing. When I was ready, I'd let her know. In the meantime, there was a whole new person waiting to be crafted. Well, cropped, touched up, and airbrushed, anyway.

So I made Claire take a picture of me with my back to the camera, my face turned to the side dramatically. She took it in black and white, so you couldn't tell that my mousy brown hair wasn't really dirty blonde or that my brown eyes weren't green.

"I don't think we should change this picture. It looks really good just as it is, you know?" Claire tried once again, more feebly this time, to dissuade me from my Photo Shop mission.

"Look, Claire," I said, exhaling. "Regardless of your feelings on my self-image problems, Olivia's profile picture can't look like me. If I'm going to try to friend the same people with two different Facebook accounts, the photos have to look different enough that no one is suspicious."

Mollified, at least for the time being, Claire pulled out her laptop to work her graphic design magic on the photo. I stood over her shoulder, giving her instructions for every single part of my body. We trimmed things away, enlarged some others (ahem), and put the curves in all the right places. Within an hour, dowdy and boring Jennifer Smith became hot, smoldering Olivia Saunders—a model/hopeful actress/diner waitress. My sister, although resistant to do so, had shaved off about 30 pounds from my frame and basically added them all to my breasts. Olivia looked nothing like me.

She was perfect, at least to me.

"Um, Jen," Claire said, studying the finished product with her head tilted to the side. "You do know who this looks like, right?"

I looked at the picture hard, squinting my eyes. All I could see was the image I'd crafted back in Dr. Brinkley's exam room. The New Jennifer that I was going to aspire to become, one day. Eventually. For now, there she was, peeking at me from over her slender shoulder.

"It looks like how I picture Olivia, Claire... What am I missing?"

Claire shook her head, looking away. "Nothing. It just reminded me of somebody..."

"Huh," I shrugged my shoulders and nudged her off my desk chair. "Can I post it now?"

"Yeah, sure. It's all ready to go," she said, still a bit distracted. I let it go, thinking she was just scrolling through her mental rolodex to place whomever Olivia's photo had reminded her of. It pleased me to see this, since that's exactly what I'd wanted: to give people the feeling that this woman was someone everyone knew or recognized from somewhere. Someone just on the edge of memory.

Of course, it didn't take long for my genius plan to start back-firing. Because Claire was already in my apartment, working at my desk, she discovered my secret stash of diet brochures from Dr. Brinkley while I was updating my fake Facebook profile.

She was "straightening up" my make-shift office and I had my back to her, clicking away on my laptop, looking for people to send friend requests to and get this project off the ground. To make it look like I was legit, I posted a bogus status update: "Off to another rehearsal for..." What would Olivia be rehearsing on a random week night? Shakespeare? Simon? Ah, I got it. "Off to another rehearsal for Noises Off!"

Olivia would play the underwear-clad Brooke, a young undiscovered actress with virtually no acting instincts. It struck me that Olivia was perfect for this role and I wondered if that's where I got the idea for her in the first place. After all, *Noises Off* was one of my favorite movies. Whatever happened to my copy of that DVD? It had to be around here somewhere.

Anyway, with my status updated, I moved on to my recent notifications and learned that three random people had accepted my friend request, bringing my friend total to a respectable 18 in record time. The new friends included Tom Payone, Duncan Montieff, and some guy named Brent Deeper, who might actually be a porn star with a name like that. His location was listed as Hollywood, CA, so I guess anything's possible.

"Hey Jen, what the heck is all this?" she asked, flipping through the disheveled stack.

"What the heck is *what?*" I tossed the question over my shoulder, my eyes locked on a long list of possible friends for Olivia to have.

"All these brochures and stuff. Yoga for Plus Size Women? Your Slow Metabolism and You? Come on, Jen, where did these come from?"

I groaned, dropping my head into my hands. I should have hidden it better. It had only been a few days since my trip to see Dr. Brinkley, but my new commitment to fitness had ended almost as soon as it had begun. Hence, my cupcake lunch. It was just like every other time I'd committed myself to fitness in the past. If Claire knew about it, there was only one thing that could happen.

"If you're trying to lose weight, why won't you let me help you?" she asked, sounding a bit hurt. I turned to her then, almost feeling bad about all the times I'd refused her help. And not just earlier that day in my kitchen.

"I'm *not* trying, I already told you. My doctor gave me those last week, okay? Just leave it alone." My voice sounded strained, but I stayed defiant under her pressuring gaze. "Put them back please."

For a few moments, Claire complied. She stacked the pamphlets back up, positioning the pile carefully on the corner of my desk, without saying a word. I watched her suspiciously as she finished clearing off the desk, dropping pens into the pen holder and dropping all of my unopened mail into its designated basket. She kept her back to me, but even so, I knew she wasn't going to stop.

Mentally, I counted down from ten. Right on cue, just as my brain thought the word *one*, she cleared her throat.

"You know," she said, with as much nonchalance as she is capable of. "I was really hoping you could finally help me tackle that quilting project I've been putting off…"

"What quilting project?"

"Remember when you were going to show me how to turn all those old t-shirts from high school into a quilt? I have a whole tote full of them in my closet and I need to get rid of them. So I was thinking, maybe if you helped me, since you were always so much better at that crafty stuff than I am…"

"Okay," I said, stretching out the last syllable. I knew that second shoe was going to drop at any moment.

"But I know you're really busy, so I wouldn't want to impose. Or, at least, I wouldn't want to feel like you were helping me for nothing, you know?"

"Uh huh..." I turned my eyes back to my laptop under the guise of working. In reality, I just kept clicking back and forth between two open windows on my screen, waiting for her to finish her belabored point.

"So maybe we could do some sort of... I don't know... *talent* exchange?"

I snapped my laptop shut quietly, raising my eyes to her once again. Claire was leaning against my clean desk, arms crossed, and apparently lost in her thoughts. As transparent as her efforts were, I really loved her right then for how hard she was trying.

"Fine, Claire. You can help me."

"Help you what?" She blinked, playing dumb.

I narrowed my eyes at her.

"Okay, okay," she caved, looking relieved and truly pleased. "You won't regret this, I promise. Just be ready to go at 6 am tomorrow. I'm picking you up and we're getting started right away."

"Tomorrow? It's Saturday," I protested.

Claire was already halfway out the front door. She turned to me, hands on her hips. "Calories don't take the weekends off, Jen. And neither do we."

CHAPTER FOUR

So in the morning, I found myself held prisoner by my sister.

"You're going to love this place," Claire said, for the fourth time, as she pulled into a parking spot in front of a local gym.

"Tom's Workout World?" I was a bit skeptical, unable to stop myself from mocking the chosen title of this hole-in-the-wall facility. Located in a rundown strip mall, where his only neighbors were a dry cleaning service and a pet grooming salon—neither of which had any customers at that particular moment, or possibly in the last five years—Tom's place was more like a workout hut and less like a *world*.

The sign was cracked, for starters, and the storefront window appeared never to have been introduced to a squeegee. I was less worried about getting a good workout during my visit than I was about the risk of contracting a foreign illness from the place.

"You seriously workout here?" I asked my sister. I couldn't quite bring myself to get out of the car. Claire, on the other hand, had already parked, turned off the engine, tied her hair into a neat ponytail, and fished our gym bags out of the back seat. She thrust mine into my lap with deliberate force.

"Come on, Complainy Pants. Let's get your sweat on."

"I hope that's all I get on me..." I muttered the words under my breath as we both popped out of Claire's little Civic, but she heard me. I wish my sister didn't have super-human ears sometimes. Lord knows, I wouldn't have heard *her*, not with my damaged hearing nerves. And because life is so unfair, I got a punch in the arm. "Oww!"

I scowled, reluctantly falling into step beside her as we neared the building. My instincts told me to stop moving, but my arm was already sore. Why challenge Claire when it was obviously so pointless?

"No more whining. I will give Tom permission to torture you for every complaint you utter."

"And why would he listen to you?" I snapped at her.

"No reason."

I caught Claire's shifty look and raised my eyebrows. She looked away, somewhere off into the distance. Interesting.

The inside of Tom's Workout World couldn't have been any more different from what I expected. From the parking lot, you'd never believe there were flat panel televisions, state-of-the-art exercise machines, and a staff of at least five super-hot trainers in here. Maybe they left the windows grimy on purpose, to keep petty criminals and Peeping Toms at bay. Ha! Toms. Well, it's a theory, I guess.

Anyway, staring around the gym, I could barely take it all in. Let's just say I felt more than a little bit out of my element at that moment

Tom himself greeted us at the front desk and I had to do a double-take. He was the most gorgeous man I had ever seen in my entire life. And I'm including the time I met George Clooney in a grocery store during his days on *ER*. That was pretty hot, but Tom is the kind of guy that makes you want to take a sculpting class. Hard, well-toned muscles from head to toe—that kind of guy. I mean, looking at him, I could see muscles that I didn't have names for. Granted, I'm not a Master's candidate for anatomy, but still. Even through a thin Tom's Workout World t-shirt, his body was visibly defined. I kind of wanted to try squeezing oranges on his pectoral muscles.

Would that even work?

I bet Tom knows. And judging from the way my sister was looking at him right then, she may know too. Ohhh, lucky Claire!

With this new information, I risked one last greedy look at Tom and promised it would be my last. He was clearly my sister's turf, and I was not the kind of girl to go violating her trust or stepping on her toes. Like Tom would ever be interested in someone like me over Claire.

Still, something kept my eyes lingering on the chiseled jaw line, the high cheekbones, and the jet black hair. I felt like I'd seen Tom somewhere before, but the memory was too distant for me to grasp. If my suppositions about him and Claire were true, then maybe I'd bumped into him at a party with her somewhere. You'd think I would have instant recall for a guy like Tom if I'd met him in public before, wouldn't you? But for some reason, I just couldn't make the connection.

While my sister and her hot trainer talked—or rather, flirted—with each other, I spotted the three of us reflected in a mirror across the room. Really, beyond any sisterly loyalty I might have felt, the view of us standing together was enough to confirm that I was not the one who would be getting anywhere past the gym with this trainer. Claire and Tom leaned in toward one another as they spoke, each one shapely and toned in all the right ways. Off to the side, there was lonely me—the slow member of the herd, left behind to find food and shelter on her own. Or maybe get picked off by a predator. All alone and vulnerable. Possibly limping.

Claire has always been the kind of big sister who casts a big shadow. I guess maybe that's why I've been eating my feelings for all these years. Such a huge shadow meant that I had to grow even bigger, just to be seen around it. I have a bad habit of taking metaphors too literally, even on a subconscious level from time to time.

Anyway, Claire is always neat, orderly, and totally put-together. She has a great job as a graphic designer for this upstart marketing company. She basically helped the owner build it up from the ground and earned her way up to Vice President in less than ten years. Claire has a show-stopping resume, a killer head of luscious hair, and a dynamite pair of long legs. Honestly, her legs would make a giraffe jealous. She was a cheerleader in high school, an honor-roll student, and one of the best soloist sopranos in the choir. I couldn't even get *in* to the choir.

Still, I was much happier to have a job on the high school newspaper, where I wrote an anonymous column about bullying in the school for two years. Beyond that, I just kept my head down and tried not to get shoved into any lockers. Where Claire Smith stood out and got noticed, her little sister was working on being invisible, as much as one girl can be.

Years later, standing in a gym next to the two fittest people I'd ever seen, I was still trying to blend with the crowd, just in a whole different way. Why was I trying to lose this weight again? Was it really because I wanted to get healthy? Because I wanted to get noticed and stand out from the crowd for the right reasons? Or because being overweight was now the thing that was drawing the attention to me and I was still desperate to blend right in?

It was a good thing I decided against that Master's in Psychology my mom wanted me to get.

"So, Jen, it's nice to meet you," Tom said suddenly, seizing my hand and shaking it. "Or do you prefer Jennifer?"

I gazed into his eyes, fighting the urge to bat my eyelashes and considered his question. Hell, he could call me Fat Chick and I would be okay with it, as long as he said it in that smooth, velvety voice of his.

"Jen's fine." I managed to squeak out the words, and Claire nudged me in the ribs.

Tom, who seemed oblivious to my blatant lust, just smiled. He probably gets that all the time from his clients anyway. "Let's get you ladies worked out."

Within an hour, I had changed my mind about this gym, this trainer, and my horrible sister, whose bad ideas just kept getting worse and worse. Seriously, how guilty would she feel when I dropped dead from Tom's impossible workout routines? Huh?

"I am going to freaking kill you, Claire." I said the words slowly, painfully, around my gasping breaths. I was not allowed to take a break to smack her, so I had to keep lifting the stupid medicine ball over my head and then down again into a squat while I cursed out my evil sister. "Why? Why am I here?"

"Shh!" Claire shook her head at me, timing her squats with mine. It was hard not to notice how much less she was sweating, how much easier this seemed to be for her. How much easier everything we'd done that day, from the two-mile treadmill run to the 50 push-ups, had been for her. "Do. Your. Squats."

Tom leaned in toward me, his face practically touching mine, and yelled. "There's no time for chit-chat in my gym!"

Since we'd begun working out together—or rather, since he'd started screaming in my face while I worked out—Tom looked gradually less appealing to me. I noticed a vein that popped out of his forehead when he got angry. Very distracting. And also, he spit on me a little whenever he screamed. Also unattractive.

Claire could keep him.

"Ten more, ladies! Move, move!" Tom paced back and forth in front of us, counting us down from ten, spitting to emphasize all the hard consonants. I sort of wanted to throw my medicine ball at his back, just to see if I could knock him over. Probably not. The man is a pure wall of muscle.

Reaching the end of the set, I dropped the medicine ball onto the mat, enjoying the satisfying thud it made against the vinyl padding. That would have left a nice welt on my trainer. Maybe next time. Tom handed us each a towel and our water bottles, let us take a few moments to recover, and then sent us down to the mats for our cool down stretches. I faced my sister as we stretched out our legs, scowling at her the whole time. It was her fault that my body hurt in places I couldn't discuss in public, that my legs felt like jelly, that I was hungry enough to eat an entire live animal. Possibly Tom himself if you left me in here long enough.

After we were finally finished with the ritualistic torture, Tom switched back to his old self almost instantly. No more scary Drill Sergeant Tom, just regular old Friendly Tom. Claire didn't seem to be even the tiniest bit fazed by this weird on/off thing he had going. Having never spent much time with a personal trainer before that day, I had to assume it was just a regular thing that happened in gyms. What happened in the gym, stayed there? Just like Vegas. That made sense to me.

Hmmm... gym culture. Maybe that should have been my sociologically topic.

I left the would-be love birds to spend some time flirting together, mostly so I could find a nice, comfy chair and sit down. My body ached from my pinky toenail all the way up to my hair follicles. I unwound my hair elastic and shook my sweaty, sticky mane loose, combing my fingers through the tangles. I didn't know my hair could feel pain, but apparently it needed to stretch out and cool down just as much as my calf muscles.

"Hey there."

I straightened up instantly, strands of sweaty hair hanging over my face like I was some sort of swamp creature. There was a male figure standing in front of me, one that could have easily been Tom, given his shape and size. As I brushed the hair from my face, I got a better look at him and his stunning smile. He was tall and muscular, which seemed to be the norm inside the Workout World, but he had kind eyes and the sort of grin you might keep running on a treadmill to reach. He must have been another trainer, given his apparel and the overall condition of his amazingly toned body. I had to wonder if these guys were all part-time Chippendales by night, and if so, where I could see them perform. Of course, I'd bring Claire along with me. What else are sisters for?

"Nice job today," he said, offering his hand. "I'm Noah, one of the other trainers. I saw you working with Tom over there."

"Yeah, he's pretty tough," I shrugged it off, because I am just that cool. "Decent workout though."

That statement was only true if almost dying three times counted as *decent* inside the gym. I wouldn't know, because I'd never been inside of a gym before. Still, Noah smiled knowingly and nodded his approval. Look how quickly I adapted to that tricky gym culture, huh? That must've been my impending sociology degree hard at work.

"I haven't seen you here before, uh…"

"Jen," I said, straightening my posture. I split my hair into a part and smoothed it down along both sides of my face. If he hadn't noticed the hearing aids yet, I wasn't about to let him now. "Don't tell anyone, but today was my first workout in… I don't know how long."

"You make it sound like you're stepping into a confessional or something," he laughed lightly. "In which case, I don't think I'm allowed to tell anyone, am I?"

"Guess not." I smiled back at him; I couldn't help myself, he was just so smiley.

"Well, Jen, I hope I get to see you around here again sometime soon." He adjusted the duffle bag on his shoulder and tucked his hands into his pockets. "I'm usually here Tuesday through Friday afternoons if you want to sign up for a session with me one of these days."

"Thanks," I had to force myself not to giggle. Had he just invited me to sweat in his general vicinity? That had never happened to me before. "I'll keep you… uh, that in mind."

Noah winked one of his dreamy eyes at me and I tried not to visibly swoon. Winking isn't something that happened to me very often either, so I found myself staring after him for a full five minutes, long after he'd exited the door, climbed into his Jeep, and pulled away.

"You okay?" I heard Claire say from somewhere nearby. Blinking, I came to and looked up at her. "Welcome back to earth. What the heck was that?"

I rubbed my eyes and stood up. "I have absolutely no idea."

Back at my apartment, it took her less than an hour to destroy my entire kitchen. In what seemed like seconds, Claire had fired up the crock pot with something healthy in it to eat for dinner in six hours. The next thing I knew, she was raiding my cabinets...again. How rude. I quickly evacuated the kitchen, choosing to hide behind my laptop screen until the dust settled. It was a full ten minutes before I heard another word from her, but the rustling and general clatter arising from my kitchen made me nervous.

Then, suddenly, it was all over. "Okay, you can come in now!"

Fearing the worst, I peered around the doorway into my little galley kitchen. I did not want to go in there. Claire knew where I kept the sharp objects. Although I didn't see any sharp objects from where I was standing, I preferred to err on the side of caution. I could see, however, that Claire had emptied the contents of my cabinets directly onto the countertops. There were three piles, neatly stacked, of all my canned goods, assorted non-perishables, and secret stash of junk food.

How did she find the good stuff? Especially after I'd re-hidden it in even better spots this time.

"So, here's the deal," she said, hands on her hips. She tossed her hair once before she continued, pointing to each pile in turn. "I've divided all your food into three categories. From now on, we will refer to these as Green Light, Yellow Light, and Red Light foods."

I crossed my arms and narrowed my gaze. The pile with all my secret food had just been dubbed "Red Light," which was either code for "not allowed" or "only acceptable in a special, brothel-heavy part of town." Neither option boded well for me.

Claire continued, unperturbed. "I want you to start concentrating on eating mostly Green Light foods, like the whole grain stuff and the canned veggies. We'll need to get more fresh produce to load up your fridge, but at least the canned stuff is a starting point." She studied the piles for a moment, before turning back to me. "So the Yellow Light foods are ones that you can have *once in a while* and the Red Light foods you should, obviously, avoid."

I stared at the Red Light pile, which included my hidden Oreo package and a bag of emergency Lays potato chips, before glowering at my very mean, very bossy sister. I knew she was trying to help me, but come on. I was a grad student. Junk food was a prerequisite. And those poor Gummy Bears would never understand why I couldn't eat them.

"I thought you wanted to get healthy, Jen." Her words were spoken calmly, not as a question but not with any significant force either. "I'm just trying to help you."

I studied my sister for a moment, from her gorgeous healthy hair to her perky bosom and down to her smooth, toned legs. If anyone knew what she was talking about in the fit and healthy department, it was Claire. I grew up with her, so I knew her good looks and a toned, fit physique hadn't just come naturally to her. She'd put in a tremendous amount of work to look this good and it was paying off. I guess I should've been paying more attention during my formative years. It might've saved me some grief. Looking at her that day, preaching to me about vegetables from my tiny kitchen, I could see how badly she wanted me to be healthy and finally happy with *myself*. Claire knew as well as I did that my cheesecake habit wasn't making me healthy or happy, and that a good change of pace might do more than just help me drop down to a new jeans size.

The one summer during my life when I actually did stick to a diet plan and lose weight, I felt good about myself. It had less to do with the actual pounds lost, or the smaller waistline, and much more to do with being disciplined. Something about sticking to a plan, doing something worthwhile just for myself, and no one else... it struck a chord with me. I had more confidence, I had more patience, and I just had *more*. Of everything. Then, to top it all off, when I looked in the mirror, I liked what I saw.

Something upset my apple cart way back then, and I'd never been able to climb back onboard. I think I got lost striving for other things—grades, friends, higher paychecks, and other such nonsense. But there was Claire—sweet, helpful Claire—willing to get me back on track and hold my hand as long as necessary. To kick my butt in the gym and slap the fork out of my hand if need be. I would be a fool to let any more time go by without listening to what she had to say.

"Hold on a second," I said, raising one finger. She raised an eyebrow, but let me dash back to my desk. I grabbed my iPad, returned to the kitchen, and dropped into one of the chairs. Finger at the ready, eager for some healthy eating tips, I nodded for her to continue.

Claire gasped, and then met my gaze with a smile. "I can't believe this is happening right now. You ready?"

"As I'll ever be," I sighed. It was one of those "now or never" moments, and I wasn't a fan of never.

CHAPTER FIVE

Claire was too smart for me. She took all of my Red Light foods to an unknown dumpster between her apartment and mine. I watched her tote my secret feel-good snacks out in a trash bag and had to force myself to stay still. It was just food. It had no power over me. None at all.

Besides, I told myself after she had finally left, there were plenty of other ways to occupy my mind that weren't related to food. Eating out of loneliness or boredom hadn't gotten me anything but a bigger waistline and a lot less self-esteem. Instead, I decided to change into some sweats and try one of those fitness programs On Demand.

One hour-long Billy Blanks, Jr. dance-a-thon later, I was both starving and exhausted. I hadn't eaten a bite of that weird health gumbo my sister made me. Taking a whiff of it, I wasn't sure that I wanted to. Choking down a few bites, I realized the best way to keep my hands busy was to keep up with Olivia's exciting social life online. It was, by far, more entertaining than my own.

Alternating between the two profiles, the difference in activity was staggering and a little bit depressing. My place in the social pecking order was becoming quite clear, thanks to this little experiment. I spent some time scanning the new friend requests Olivia had received. My "hot" photo was working wonders to broaden her appeal, garnering an impressive 50 or so requests in little more than a day. Eager to focus on the research aspect and stop feeling sorry for myself, I got out my notebook and started writing. Lost in thought and furious note-taking, I almost missed the blinking message notification on my computer's task bar.

Ooh! A message!

As I clicked it open, my entire body went cold. It was Sean. *The* Sean. I had to close my eyes a moment, take a few deep breaths to keep from passing out, before I could look at my computer screen again. Yes, it was him all right, twelve years later and looking as amazing as he ever had.

Sean O'Dwyer—a man with a name as Irish as mine was boring—had sent me a message. Well, he'd sent Olivia a message. I clicked on his picture, pulling up the photo of a normal-looking man who seemed out of place amidst all the model-like shots of my other virtual friends. Sean O'Dwyer is a nice-looking young guy, around my age, and in much better shape than me.

But I wasn't going to think about that just then, because it depressed me.

I examined Sean's photo, a picture of him with his thumbs hooked in his pockets, standing on a beach somewhere. He looked muscular, but not overly so, and had a carefree posture and light smile on his face. Sunglasses and a backwards hat, paired with a navy blue t-shirt and a pair of board shorts, made him look like he was some sort of beach bum or surfer. Don't those people get eaten by sharks?

The thought of Sean getting eaten by a shark made me a little sick, so I took another bite of health gumbo to distract my stomach.

Moving back to his message, I just took it all in, one word at a time.

Dear Olivia –

I hope you don't mind me being forward and reaching out to you like this. You remind me of a classmate I had back in junior high. I'm terrible with names, but your picture looks really familiar to me. When you popped up as a suggested friend, I figured it didn't hurt to take a chance and see! If you are her, and we did go to school together, I'd love to reconnect.

Anyway, how are things? Hope everything is going well. Seems like you've been keeping very busy since we last saw one another. Best of luck with your modeling career!

Sean

A classic case of mistaken identity. It was almost funny: I created someone completely fictional and managed to find an actual, real-life person who thought he knew her. What a special skill I seemed to have.

But then again, he did know her. Well, *me*. Could it be that somewhere in the back of Sean's subconscious, he remembers me from our days in school together? I never thought he had even noticed me before, but if my altered photo reminded him of a classmate... chances were good it was *me* he was reminded of. Right?

Tangled in my own web of logic, I wasn't sure what to do, how to proceed. Here's the boy—now grown to a man—that I had always been in love with, but had never thought to ever pursue. The photo of me, this new person Olivia whom I aspired to become, had attracted him after all this time. What could I do?

I read the message a few more times through, tapping my fingers idly on my desk. I knew Olivia wasn't real and that I had absolutely no obligation to respond to her messages. Still, there was no way on earth that I would let a message from *the* Sean O'Dwyer sit unanswered. I glanced at my notebook, waiting patiently nearby for more jotted thoughts and observations. Which I could only get if I took the plunge. Besides, corresponding as my fake identity could really help me explore a whole new angle of my thesis.

And how else could I keep his attention? It's not like I could tell him, *Oh this is a fake profile. You really wanted to talk to Jen... here's the link to her profile.* I'd never hear from him ever again if I sent him to my profile, where my photo was more of a work-in-progress than a satisfying end result.

But was this ethical? I thought about it for a moment, regretting the absence of a cat once more. A cat would know what to do, or at least look like he was listening while I talked about it out loud. Cats have always struck me as very fixed in their morals. Fine pillars of virtue, if you will. I imagined a fluffy orange tabby sitting at my feet, prim and proper, judging me with its beady little eyes.

Stupid cat. Didn't he know how badly I needed to get an A on this project?

So I typed:

Dear Sean –

I think I remember you from school as well, although it's been a really long time! I've done some traveling since, and met so many people; it's sometimes hard to keep names and faces straight.

Olivia would totally play it this cool, even if she were the one doing mental cartwheels around the house at the mere appearance of Sean O'Dwyer's name in her message box. So I kept going, as nonchalant as possible. Claire always said it was good not to look too eager when talking to a guy... so here goes nothing.

I just moved back to Boston last year after hopping from school to school in cities all over the world. With my dad in the military, we never really settled down in one place, but here I am now, trying to make Boston my home again. Are you still living in the area?

Olivia

I had to backspace over "Jennifer" two times before I got my fake name right. Amateur. Then I hit send and watched the screen fade back to my profile page... just seconds before I realized my fatal misstep.

Are you still living in the area? Come on! What was I thinking? The point was to see how he reacted to things, not invite him to have an adult sleepover with me some time. As much as I might like that, I didn't think it would be easy to convince Sean that I was actually Olivia, not until this weight went vamoose for good.

Olivia, the giant slut, was already having a bad influence on me!

Sean, apparently, liked to hang out online about as much as I did and so I got his reply in mere minutes. I also confirmed my worst fears.

Olivia –

Yes, I'm still living in the area, working with a landscaping company downtown. I love this city too much to move away! Maybe we should get together and I could give you a tour of all my favorite places to visit in Boston. I'm sure you could use a refresher. Besides, it would be great to have an excuse to see the sights myself.

If you're interested, let me know when you're free next week.

Sean

What in God's name am I doing? I hit delete so fast, it made my head spin. And then I wiped my sweaty palms back and forth on my pant legs. Back and forth. Like I was trying to start a fire or something.

The point of this experiment was to stay virtual, not arrange fake tours of the city I'd lived in since birth. No more contact with Sean.

No.

No more.

Don't even think about it.

When the time came for my second trip to Tom's Workout World, I felt more prepared for what was going to happen. Not only had I been doing some work at home on my own, but I was also properly dressed for the occasion. I wore special sweat-wicking clothing, a fancy hair band to keep fly-aways out of my face, and a new pair of shoes. I considered it all an investment in my future fitness. Even Claire seemed impressed with this show of commitment.

Tom, on the other hand, was about as impressed as I am when I eat my special "diet breakfasts." He screamed and yelled as usual, while Claire went about her business like the guy she liked didn't have a split personality disorder. I, on the other hand, found myself distracted by that bulging vein and covered in spittle. Just disgusting.

This time, we hauled ass on the elliptical machines for a bit, swung some really heavy ropes up and down, and then did military-style sit-ups. I thought I was going to throw up mid-way through the sit-ups, but somehow, I kept it together and made it through. I have to admit, if I could stand up and walk away from Tom's workouts, I felt *damn* good about myself.

That day, it was rough going for a few minutes, but eventually I found my footing and changed my clothes in the locker room. Claire stayed out on the floor, flirting with Tom again. She didn't need a change or a shower, probably, since she barely broke a sweat during all of that. Sometimes working out with Claire made me feel like a lazy three-toed sloth when I compared the two of us.

For my own sake, I tried not to compare myself to Claire. Neither in the gym nor anywhere else, for that matter. Life was much happier that way.

In the locker room, I dressed in my sweat-free clothes, a pair of jeans and a holey *Buffy the Vampire Slayer* t-shirt I couldn't quite part with, and headed back out onto the floor to find Claire. On my way, I passed a pair of toned, muscly female trainers comparing notes on gym patrons they couldn't stand. Nearby, there was an older woman working out with a guy that could've been Tom's younger brother, based on his attitude. And then, at the treadmills, I saw Noah again.

He was wearing a plain navy blue t-shirt and a pair of gray jersey shorts—the kind of attire I'm sure most people would love to wear to work. On the treadmill, I saw a scrawny guy struggling to keep up his pace. Rather than take the harsh Tom-like approach, Noah was cheering him on.

"That's it, Jim. Keep it up! Thirty more seconds. Twenty-nine..." Noah talked loud enough to be heard over the whirring of the machine, but he didn't scream.

And instead of wincing, treadmill-bound Jim seemed really motivated to keep moving. They meshed—trainer and trainee. Jim got from Noah the tactics he needed to stay focused.

My trainer, on the other hand, was not exactly gelling with me. Not like *that*. I guess we all have our own way of being reached. If I'd learned anything from my two gym training sessions, it was that "my way" was not to be screamed at.

Plus, Noah just seemed so relaxed and... cheerful. It sort of made me want to walk over there and hug him.

Just as I was about to resume my search for Claire, Noah turned and spotted me watching him. We shared an awkward moment of eye contact across the gym and then he gave me a little wave. I waved back—careful not to look like a child who'd just spotted Santa at the mall—and used the moment as my excuse to move on. If I stood there any longer, he might come over and talk to me.

Right then, who knows how much I'd have been gushing over him? I couldn't be trusted.

So I wound my way around various pieces of gym equipment to the front desk where there was no sign of my sister. Since she was my ride home, it was kind of important that I find her. I checked the parking lot and spotted her car, so I knew she was somewhere inside still. Good to know I hadn't been abandoned. I mean, leave it to Claire to ditch me in a gym as an extreme method of either fitness motivation or torture. Or both.

I checked all the little alcoves of the gym, anywhere that wasn't within my direct line of sight, but I came up empty. I revisited the ladies' locker room, careful to keep my eyes straight ahead as I walked past Noah again. The locker room was empty, so I poked my head into the men's room to call out their names really fast. Nothing there either.

Just as I was about to give up, I turned on my heel and almost crashed into a sculpted male body in a navy blue t-shirt.

"Come here often?" Noah asked with one eyebrow raised.

I blinked at him a couple of times. "To the gym?"

"To the men's locker room."

Busted. "Oh!" I smoothed my still-damp hair down over my hearing aids and tried not to blush. "No, I was looking for my sister."

"Does *she* come here often?"

My nervous laughter sounded forced, high-pitched. I cringed.

"It's Claire, right?" As he said this, Noah stepped into the locker room to do a quick scan for me. He came out shaking his head.

"No, I'm Jennifer," I said, utterly crestfallen at having my name confused for hers. Again.

"I know *that*. I meant your sister is Claire."

"Oh…uh, yeah." This cheered me a little bit.

"She comes in here all the time, works out with Tom, right? About 5-foot-8, dirty blonde hair?"

I nodded, impressed by his recall. And his tactful way of not saying "super-hot, long legs, big boobs." It was almost refreshing.

"Yeah, I know her. And I think I can help you find her." He put his hands on his hips, considering me for a moment. And then he started walking.

I followed Noah back through a set of double doors labeled "Employees Only." As soon as I crossed the threshold, I started checking over my shoulder, as though I could get arrested for trespassing or something. Paranoia is such a bummer sometimes.

"They come back here together, once in a while," Noah said, thumbing toward a door that was Tom's office, judging from the plaque. "They don't know that I know that, though, okay?"

"Oh… uh, thanks," I muttered. Noah waved to me again, and then headed back the way we came in, toward the men's locker room. I watched him walk all the way back down the darkened corridor, mesmerized by his perfect form. It almost wasn't natural, how good he looked.

The world of gym culture was a remarkable place indeed...

Shaking it off, I turned back to Tom's office door and knocked deliberately. It wasn't a habit of mine to interrupt or try to catch my sister in the act, so to speak, but I needed to get home in time to get my stuff together for class this afternoon. When no one opened the door right away, I held my ear close to it—not quite pressing it against the wood, because contact makes my hearing aids buzz with feedback—and listened. Rustling, low voices, a chair scraping across the concrete floor. I couldn't make out any words, or be completely sure who was speaking, thanks to my stupid hearing loss. But I could at least say there were one male and one female in there.

When the door finally swung open, I was faced with Tom's unusually smooth forehead. Whatever he had been doing in there, it wasn't a private training session.

"Oh, Jen, hi," he said, forcing a smile. "Claire and I were just finishing up our training schedule for the next two months. I hope you'll be joining us for some of the sessions."

I didn't miss the subtle way he drew a line in the sand with the word "some," for the record.

He opened the door wider and Claire stepped around him into the corridor with me. She looked a little flushed, but otherwise normal. It was hard to say for sure what I'd really interrupted, but I had my own opinions on the matter.

"Thanks again, Tom," she said stiffly, her eyes daring from me to him and back. If Claire hadn't been intimately entangled with that man just a few minutes' previous, I was the Queen of England. "See you on Tuesday for the..."

"Race."

"Yeah," she smiled. "You better watch out for me. I'll be waiting for you at the finish line. See you then!"

For the entire car ride home, I badgered my sister for information. She stoically resisted every attempt I made, her lips pressed tightly together.

"What's really on Tuesday?" I asked, poking her in the arm.

"It's a 5K, Jen. We're running it for charity and we've got a little wager between us. Just some friendly competition." She kept her eyes on the road.

"What's the wager for? Huh? Sensual body massages?"

Without looking at me, Claire swatted my leg. "Stop it! It's not like that."

"Ouch! I don't know why you won't just tell me, Claire. What's the big deal?"

When we finally pulled into my parents' driveway, she turned to me calmly and said, "Tom's just a friend. There's nothing to tell."

I'm sorry, but I had to call shenanigans on that.

After class that afternoon, I met with Dr. Chase to outline the parameters of my social networking experiment. I'd submitted a one-page proposal a few days earlier, detailing the real profile versus the fake profile experiment, as well as some of my early findings. The meeting was just a formality, or so I hoped, to get final approval to go ahead with my research study and start writing my final paper.

"You're taking this in an interesting direction," Dr. Chase said, unfolding my proposal paper and scanning it quickly. "Especially with the blind friend requests. What do you expect to achieve with that?"

"I'm hoping that will show the power of anonymity on the internet. My theory is, as long as you look good in your photo, people will blindly trust you and accept your friend requests. Basically, you can be anyone you want on the internet and, thus, control how people respond to you."

"Did you come up with this?"

"It was a collaborative effort. My sister's been dying to help me come up with something really daring," I rolled my eyes, but smiled at the memory of my 'photo shoot' with Claire. "She did the editing on my photo too."

"I hope you don't mind," Dr. Chase continued, smoothing the hair into her loose bun. "But I took the liberty of looking up the profile for Olivia Saunders when you submitted your write-up. Interesting stuff there, Jen."

I shifted nervously in my chair.

"Now, as far as the project is concerned, are you positive there won't be any legal ramifications of friending at random and posing as someone else?"

"Well, the worst that can happen, from what I've gathered, is that the account would be suspended for adding too many strangers as friends. But that rarely happens, judging from some of the people I've encountered so far."

"No fines or penalties or anything?" Dr. Chase was just being cautious, I could tell from her tone.

"As long as I'm not impersonating someone real, I'm good."

She nodded, then handed me the proposal back. "You should keep an eye on the main news sites. See if there are any real-life cases you can follow to further your study."

"Actually, there are a couple already, mostly people posing as ex-boyfriends and stuff. But I saw one report where the FBI was actually using fake Facebook profiles to watch and monitor known criminals. I'm not the FBI, obviously, but it makes me feel better to know law enforcement has been doing this too." I tried to laugh a little to break the tension.

Dr. Chase smiled back. "You should learn more about that for the paper. Talk about how criminals post so liberally online and don't realize how easily they can get busted that way."

"So am I good to go?" I stood up, tucking the paper into the front pocket of my messenger bag.

"I think so," she said, eying me. "Just, Jennifer..?"

I looked up at her.

"Try to remember that this is just a project. I've seen too many students get wrapped up in their research and go over the deep-end. It's just a project and your research is meant to be a temporary thing. Don't get carried away with this fake profile business, okay? Especially pitting her against you online, there's a chance of losing yourself in the shuffle."

"I think I can handle it, Dr. C. It's only for now, and then I'll delete the entire thing. I'm not actually *playing* Olivia; I'm just using the name as a vehicle." But even as I said the words, I heard the false note in my voice. Aside from talking to Sean, I wasn't actually pretending to be Olivia. Not really.

Dr. Chase seemed to hear the truth in my voice too, given her skeptical look. She watched me for a moment before nodding. "Just keep it in mind," she said.

As I stepped out of her office into the main foyer of the sociology department, I shook her words off. I mean, it was only for a few months. And Olivia would stay strictly online. I'd pretended to be different people before and that hadn't hurt anyone. How was this any different from a regular game of childhood dress up?

CHAPTER SIX

Meanwhile, back on the internet, another influx of accepted friend requests waited for me in my notifications that night. Another five random men who had received Olivia's friend request, taken one look at her picture, and accepted her as a new friend, no questions asked. They didn't know her, probably didn't have anything in common with her, but that didn't seem to matter in the slightest. A pretty face, hot body, and the protected anonymity of social networking facilitated the easiest friend-making process a girl like me had ever experienced. Of course, I was only experiencing it because I was hiding behind the shield of a made-up identity, but still. Easy peasy.

So far my alter-ego had collected a whopping 94 friends, without even breaking a sweat. The long—and growing—list gave me a quiet thrill. Was this how pretty people felt? Or was this so easy to do just because of the virtual aspect of this experience? I grabbed my notebook and started jotting down some of these half-thoughts and questions, all fodder for my planned research paper. Less than two weeks into my project, this impromptu idea was already paying off.

I scanned through the list of my new acquaintances, or rather, the people I had snowed into believing my fake self was a live human being. Most of them were male, unsurprisingly, but there were a scattered few females throughout the list. While I was lost in a scrolling sea of headshot photographs and names that seemed just about as real as Olivia Saunders, my dinner grew cold beside me.

Then, out of the blue, an instant message popped up. It was Sean O'Dwyer, who hadn't heard back from me since his tour invitation, but apparently, didn't seem to mind being blown off. Or maybe he just didn't take a hint very well.

His opening line was totally innocuous, and revealed nothing about either his hint-taking skills or feelings about being ditched. "Hey Olivia! How's it going?"

I grimaced at my computer screen, then at my bowl of cold health-food sludge, and back at my computer screen. Talking to a guy in person was hard for me to do, but online? This would be a new experience for me. Email was simpler, because of the delay, but this live chat situation was sure to be a bit more stressful. It wasn't like I could mull over my response for an hour or so. I was talking live. To a guy. Who was mildly attractive. And thought I was some hot model he could rescue from the confusing streets of Boston.

He was also a guy I'd been lusting over since I hit puberty.

As my impulsive brain fought to slam my laptop closed and bolt from my apartment, my rational brain knew this was an experience I would need to chart for research purposes. It was for this reason—and this reason alone, obviously—that I engaged him in conversation, and then copied and pasted our entire exchange into a Microsoft Word document. Thus, it remains preserved in its original format:

SEAN: Hey Olivia! How's it going?
OLIVIA: Great! Keeping busy. How are you?
SEAN: Just got back from vacation.
OLIVIA: Nice! Where'd you go?
SEAN: Visiting my sister in California. She has a house near the beach—lucky bitch. LOL Anyway, back to the daily grind for me on Monday. Not looking forward to it.
OLIVIA: Hahahaha. Landscaping, right?

SEAN: Yeah. I'm a project manager, so at least I don't have to shovel anything. LOL
OLIVIA: It's been so hot this fall, that would be awful. I bet you just sit idly by and drink spiked lemonade while they do all the work, right?
SEAN: I wish! Anyway, what are you up to?

Sitting at home on my computer, trying to pretend I have a life?

OLIVIA: Working on a play, plus a few photo shoots here and there.
SEAN: That's great. It's nice you can find so many jobs in an industry like that. I hear it's tough.
OLIVIA: It can be. But not as tough as sipping spiked lemonade.
SEAN: Hahahaha. I'll switch with you any time! So what else do you do with your time? That is, if you ever get any free time!
OLIVIA: I like to cook, I guess. And sometimes I visit my uncle's farm where I keep my horse.

Lies, all lies.

SEAN: Awesome. I don't really know anyone that rides horses. I always wanted to learn.
OLIVIA: Maybe I could teach you to ride sometime.

Sometimes I want to slap myself across the face as hard as I can.

SEAN: Is there any chance you're free next weekend? I'd love a riding lesson. <wink>

It was somewhere around here that I had to step away from my laptop and walk a circle around my apartment. Sean was polite, seemed genuinely interested in my fake job and fake interests. We were chatting away like old friends catching up, except for my deception. Something in the pit of my stomach just didn't feel right about all of this. He really wanted to be friends. How could I do this to someone?

I sat back down and typed as tactful a response as I could think of: "Sorry, Sean. Have a shoot this weekend, out of town. Maybe some other time."

His answer was equally nice and polite. "Have a great time! Hope it's somewhere nice to visit so you can do some vacationy things!"

How cute was that? Fighting with myself not to encourage him any further, I made up a lie about needing to get to bed early and signed off. I dumped my mushy dinner into the sink, ran the disposal, and headed to the bathroom to get ready for bed.

My little two-bedroom apartment was the perfect size for someone like me, who didn't do much in the way of entertaining guests. I had enough space for a couch, a couple of bookshelves for all my textbooks and related sociological reading, and a two-person table. My bedroom housed my full-size bed and one dresser, plus my comfy reading chair. It was all I'd ever needed and, aside from the fact that it was attached to my parents' house, it was the perfect set up for me at that point in my life. Especially once I'd gotten my mother to stop coming in to tuck me into bed every night. I guess some old habits die hard.

Teeth brushed, pajamas on, I turned out the light and climbed into my bed. I really wanted to let myself get swept away in this Olivia thing, but I knew that in the light of day, I would still be Jennifer.

The next few days flew by in all the activity of gym trips, friend requests, and healthy meals. After a full week of Claire-enforced diet and exercise, it was time for my first weigh-in. She'd made me climb onto a scale the previous Sunday and I still hadn't quite forgiven her for the cruel and unusual punishment. Doing it again so soon was not something I was quite ready for.

"Can't I wait another week so I can get a bigger result? I think that would really help to keep me motivated. I mean, if I don't get a big number this week, what if I—"

"Cut the crap, Jen, and get on the scale."

Claire has always had this weird ability to make me do things just with the power of her voice. I never understood it, and yet, I never fought her either.

So I shrugged off my sweater, handed it to her, and stepped onto the scale. I closed my eyes tightly, too nervous to look. If this number was too small a change from the previous week, I would probably just quit like every other time. It wasn't that I expected immediate, overnight success. I just needed to know when I checked in with that scale that something was going to be different. To know that all of the pain and each one of those Oreos I denied myself was somehow worthwhile. Why couldn't I just trade in a half-pound of weight loss for every donut I passed up? That would be so much more motivating!

The scale did its thing with Claire watching and me nauseous, my eyes still closed. After a moment of painful silence, she slapped my arm.

"Open your eyes! Look, Jen!"

My eyes went to her first, and I was a bit taken aback by her look of total shock. Nervously, I glanced at the scale. Mostly out of curiosity. Had I *gained* weight after all of that? No! A number almost four pounds less than my previous week's weight stared me in the face. I could hardly believe my eyes, so I rubbed them and looked again. Yup, that was right.

"Holy cow," I said, a bit in awe.

"I know! Aren't you excited?" Claire jumped up and down, clapping her hands. I stepped off the scale and hugged her. A moment like that, that's what sisters are really for.

"Oh my God, Claire!" I had to wipe a few tears from my eyes, I was so overwhelmed. "I can't believe that just happened."

"See? It's all gonna pay off. Stick with me, kid, and we'll hit your goal in no time. We're already ten-percent of the way there!"

Slinging one arm around my shoulders, Claire guided me out of the bathroom and into the kitchen for lunch, talking about our next big plans together and how much weight I should expect to lose in the next few weeks, now that I'd dropped some of the initial "water weight."

It felt good to be here in this mental space again, to be working on the new me. To be working toward a goal. I was actually proud of myself for doing something for *me*. Not for a grade, not for a raise, not for someone else's praise. Just for Jennifer Smith.

With all that excitement and newness swirling around me during those days, it struck me as odd to have to do something as mundane as go to class. It was kind of like being a kid again, watching a really awesome commercial for a toy you just had to have, only to have that commercial fade directly into the five o'clock news or something. Snore.

Still, as I thought this each and every weekday morning, I still managed to choke down an on-the-fly (but healthy) breakfast and go about my daily routine. Most girls wake up and shower, style their hair, put on some makeup, and get dressed. But for me, mornings look a little bit different.

First of all, my alarm clock is not the typical kind that most people wake up to every day. Mine has a special bed shaking feature that helps me to get up in the morning. Being hearing impaired, I can't just rely on the irritating beep of the alarm. While that noise grates on me just as much as the next gal, sometimes it isn't loud enough to hear... especially if I've burrowed my way under the covers, as usual. So my alarm buzzes, shakes the bed, and all but shoves me onto the floor.

Sometimes I think I'd be better off trading it in for a "hearing ear" dog, as I call them, who could just lick my face or something. That would at least be more pleasant, if less hygienic.

Anyway, once I'm up, it's not just coffee that I need to get going. If I want to hear anything at all, I've got to wipe down my hearing aids, scrape out the wax from inside those tiny ear holes, and test the batteries. Trust me; it's worth testing them every morning. There's nothing worse than having one hearing aid shut off in the middle of a class, while driving, at a movie, or somewhere else inconvenient—which is pretty much everywhere. Well, I guess, having them both shut off is the only thing that would be worse.

See, without my hearing aids, I sometimes feel like I'm in a crowded mall. Everyone is talking around me and it's noisy, I can hear things, but I can't quite distinguish any of the words or even the voices. It's all there, echoing around me, but too far out of my grasp. Or it's traveling towards my ears, just landing somewhere around them instead of hitting my ear drums. I *can* hear, but it doesn't sound very good at all.

So after I stumble out of the shower—the only real time I spend awake without my hearing aids is when I'm in the water—I get to work preparing my communication lifeline to the rest of the world. While other girls are stressing over mascara smudges, I'm worrying about why my earwax seems to have doubled in quantity. Then, when I'm ready to go, that's when I look in the mirror and think to myself, *Gee… one of these days I should get up earlier so I have time to wear mascara.*

Then I go to class.

Class time those days was, obviously, made better by the use of my iPad to chart my progress online as Olivia Saunders. During one of Dr. Chase's many lectures that week, I learned that I had officially reached the "friend recommendations" stage of the experiment. Meaning, total strangers who had become my virtual friends on Facebook had begun to suggest "people I may know" among their own friends. They were passing me on and helping me to connect with more and more people, bringing my total up over 300.

Flipping back to my own profile, on the other hand, showed that not all Facebook profiles were created equal. Of the more than 200 'blind' friend requests I had sent out as plain old Jennifer Smith, only 26 had accepted—mostly normal-looking women like myself with regular interests like reading, baking, and playing Monopoly. All of the hot guys who snatched up the opportunity to friend Olivia seemed to be ignoring my real profile's requests.

Well, who wants to be friends with those guys anyway?

As I scrolled through my notifications for the influx of new friends, however boring they might have been, one name caught my attention above the others. If I hadn't been in class, I might have slapped myself.

Noah Wayland, trainer extraordinaire.

Well, it didn't say the part about being a trainer extraordinaire—obviously. I added that part myself when I read the name in my head. All the same, there was his dimpled profile picture, smiling back at me from the screen of my iPad. I knew I was blushing and it needed to stop before Dr. Chase noticed. I took a deep breath, paid attention to her lecture long enough to get the basic idea, and then turned back to Noah's profile.

He'd sent me a note along with the friend request: "Thought I could keep an eye on you online. Don't worry... my policy of trainer confidentiality is still good on the internet." And then he added a little winking smiley face at the end of it. No signature or anything, as though we were the kind of friends that needed no formalities to stand between them.

My head spun at the thought. Because, up until about five minutes before then, I hadn't even known that Noah and I were friends at all.

"All right, Jennifer?" Dr. Chase's voice cut into my thoughts, sending the room spinning around me. I forced my eyes to focus on her.

"Fine, Dr. C," I offered a weak smile, embarrassed that the rest of the class was now staring at me. Lyla squinted at me from across the classroom, trying to show some concern. I gave her the tiniest shake of my head that I could manage.

As Dr. Chase resumed her lecture, the attention shifted from me back to note-taking for most of the other students. Struck by an idea, however, I couldn't quite jump into the lecture just yet. Instead, I accepted Noah's request and sent a light-hearted message back to him: "Are you sure you know me? There are about a thousand Jennifer Smiths out there, you know." I added my own winking smiley so he would know I was kidding and not panic and unfriend me. How awkward would that be?

Meanwhile, the lecture had shifted into a discussion again, something about human rights in today's world or something. I hoped Dr. Chase would just leave me out of this one, since my brain felt a lot like Jell-O right now and couldn't be trusted to spit out any reliable information whatsoever.

Besides, my final project had absolutely zero to do with human rights anyway.

CHAPTER SEVEN

A month into my Master's project and three weeks into my exercise plan, I was starting to hit my stride. Olivia had racked up a total of 353 friends in that short span of time. And I had lost almost 10 pounds. Things were moving along well, all in the right direction for a change.

I was almost suspicious.

But it felt too good to be so busy and so successful all at the same time, so I decided to just keep going and not think about it. I'd been visiting Tom's Workout World three times a week, doing yoga DVDs on alternating days in my tiny living room, and eating a strict diet of Green Light foods. Sometimes I snuck a Yellow Light food in there, but not often. The number going down, down, down on the scale was too thrilling to let a Yellow or Red Light food binge ruin things. I was actually choosing to ignore the vending machines on campus, navigating straight to the salad bar in the cafeteria, and passing up on the carb-loaded dinners my mother kept trying to force-feed me. Claire was helping with that part, too, since my mother is a special breed of stubborn.

Of course, I leave that part out as I recap the story for my mother, who is hanging on my every word at this point.

And as far as the internet thing was concerned, I had to admit my alter-ego was helping me stay away from junk food. I guess I just needed something to keep my brain and hands occupied. I'd been reading a lot of articles about social networking, media and technology, and modern communication on Google Scholar, loading up my iPad with links and notes, and trying out new ways to connect with people.

Olivia joined some groups too. One for horseback riders, one for lovers of French cuisine, another for models with acting aspirations. There really is something for everyone on Facebook. I bet my actual profile might benefit from joining some groups or "liking" a few things here or there. If nothing else, at least this sociology experiment would teach me a thing or two about social networking. It couldn't be all bad, right?

Not that this project wasn't without its bad points too, or at least, its unsavory ones. I had to repress my gag reflex that night as I navigated through a string of distasteful conversation openers in my message box. Highlights included:

"You're so hot! How old are you?"

"Please post more photos… wearing less clothing!"

"You look familiar… Did I meet you at the Playboy mansion that one time?"

Please, people. Disgusting, unimaginative, and just downright wrong. When guys think you're gorgeous, is this how they talk to you? Having never fielded a pick-up line before, either online or in person, I didn't really have a frame of reference. I took note of the comments, deleted the messages so I didn't barf on my keyboard, and let the mouse hover over Sean's picture on my Friends list.

I knew I shouldn't be talking to him, because it was too risky and totally unfair to him. But compared to the other guys whose comments I'd just barely been able to read while keeping my lunch in my stomach, Sean was so different. He didn't belong grouped in with these losers. But it had been so long since we'd known each other… How could I really know what kind of person he was? You could be anyone you wanted to be online. And with me being such a poser myself, who was I to judge?

More importantly, who was I to try to start something with a guy like Sean?

Like the weather in New England, my resolve wavered easily from extreme to extreme. If I gave myself enough time, I knew I'd change my mind. Sure enough, as I updated my real profile photo that night with a shot of me and Claire from the previous weekend, I found I couldn't stop staring at myself. Sure, I still had a long way to go, but the Jennifer Smith in this picture was starting to look different. She was starting to shape up a little, smile some more. She was getting closer and closer every day to that airbrushed photo of Olivia. I got a chill just thinking about how much closer and closer I was inching toward this ideal.

So when Sean messaged me again that evening, I could only blame the false bravado my changing appearance gave me for my actions. It had been a while since we'd spoken, and I couldn't be sure if he'd lost interest or if he was being cautious around me because I'd come across as *too* casual. Knowing nothing about flirting etiquette or how to keep a man's attention, I was at a total loss. Message him? Post on his wall? Leave him alone?

I had no idea what I was doing. So, just for a moment, I imagined myself as Claire and tried to figure out how she would handle a situation like this. She, I knew from experience, would do something simple to reignite contact and, thus, interest. Then an idea hit me.

Carefully, I scrolled through some of Sean's recent pictures from his visit to his sister's place in California. Sean on the beach, in a bathing suit, shirtless, tanned and glistening and... Yeah, this wasn't exactly helping me to focus. I clicked through a few more until I spotted an innocuous picture of him with his arm around a girl that I took to be his sister and "liked" it.

There... now he'd know I visited his profile, seen his pictures, and cared enough to click a button. What did that mean, exactly? To me, not a whole lot. But given my experiences with others online, it could be considered a big deal if you were waiting to hear from someone. Satisfied, although a bit puzzled by social networking culture, I decided to step away from his profile before something bad happened and I screwed things up for me... er, Olivia.

Man, dating is hard.

I sighed and closed my laptop. It was time to get going anyway. I didn't want to be late for my workout. A statement, which, as I thought it, just sounded plain bizarre inside of my head.

I met Claire, as usual, in front of Tom's Workout World. She had been an angel during the previous three weeks of exercise, joining me for every one of my thrice weekly workouts. Of course, she was already so toned before we started that these workouts were just maintenance for her, but it was really nice to have a sweat buddy. And Claire was a nice enough sister never to boast about how many more sit-ups she could do than I could.

When we walked inside, it was the first time that we weren't greeted at the front desk by Tom. Instead, another familiar face smiled at us. I hadn't forgotten about Noah, but I hadn't really talked to him in a couple of weeks. I'd begun to think it was a fluke that he'd even talked to me at all and pushed it from my mind. That day, however, I was feeling good about my 10 pound weight loss, my newfound cardio endurance, and my hot workout clothes. Well, they were kinda hot, anyway. As hot as Jennifer Smith can manage, anyway.

"Hey Noah," I smiled back at him, determined to exude confidence in every word and movement. If Claire was surprised about this at all, she didn't let on.

"Good to see you again."

I nodded to him then introduced my sister as though Noah and I were old pals. Yeah, we went way back... a whole three weeks.

"Where's Tom today?" Claire finally asked, once the introductions were over. I glanced around the gym but saw no sign of the hard-muscled owner. When my eyes found their way back to Claire's face, I noticed the concern wound through her features.

"He took a few days off this week. Some family stuff or something," Noah shrugged, oblivious to my sister's worried grimace.

"Well, I hope everything's okay," I offered, more for Claire's benefit than for Noah's.

"I'm sure it is. He didn't seem upset." Noah stepped out from behind the desk and gestured toward the treadmills. "Shall we?"

While Claire seemed reluctant to comply, I was beside myself with glee. Finally, I was getting the chance to work with a trainer who wasn't a maniac with a multiple-personality disorder. If Noah was as calm as I'd seen him demonstrate with his other clients before, I might actually take some enjoyment from the day's activities. It also didn't hurt that I feel like I was betraying my sister by staring at my trainer's ass.

Speaking of which, Noah's was even *better* than Tom's. I didn't know that was even possible.

We jumped right into some cardio and I found myself motivated to do even more mileage today than normal. As expected, working out with Noah was a lot like working out with Tom, except that I found myself to be in a much, much better mood. He didn't have a weird vein bulging out of his forehead. He didn't spit in my face every time he screamed. In fact, he didn't really scream that much at all. I guess I didn't give him much of a reason to scream at me, since I was pushing myself harder than I ever had before. Claire, on the other hand, seemed to be doing the bare minimum. And still, Noah's attention was fixed on me.

For the first time in my life, I didn't really mind being the center of someone's attention at all. Not if it was going to keep me on point and help me shed these extra pounds. This was the kind of attention I knew better than to let bother me. Almost in a trance, I let him direct me from the treadmill to the weight lifting area and got to work.

"Come on, Jen, fifteen more. You can do this. One! Two!" He spoke loudly enough for me to hear above the weight machine without screaming. I'd long since forgotten that, with my hair in a ponytail, he could probably see my hearing aids. It was nice not to be thinking about them for a change.

"Come on! Three, four..." The sound of Noah's voice counting out my reps provided the focus my tired muscles needed.

I pushed through with a fiery burst of energy. I had no idea where it came from, but I used it to my advantage, ignoring the burning sensation in my muscles, reveling in the thought of being sexy enough to actually date a guy like Sean O'Dwyer someday. As I hit six, then seven reps, I watched Noah in front of me, his eyes transfixed on my arms, studying my form. He was going to be the one to help me do this, not Tom.

Eight, nine. Aside from the hot, hot, *smoldering* hot body, Noah is actually a really good looking guy. That's not always the case with these gym rat types, you know. But he's got those crazy dimples and these really bright blue eyes that I couldn't stop staring into. Noah keeps his hair fairly short in a style that seems appropriate, given his career, and it's a nice sandy, brown color that works well with his medium skin tone.

Ten. I also appreciated that he didn't seem to be the type of guy to spend hours in a tanning bed or something, just someone with a naturally moderate skin pigment. Eleven. Like he had Italian or Greek or something mixed into his lineage.

Twelve. Totally normal, totally natural. Except for the fact that his muscles were... gigantic.

As I had the thought, my eyes were already making their full scope exploration of my trainer's body. He was so focused on counting out my reps that he, fortunately, did not seem to notice me molesting him with my eyes. Thirteen, fourteen. It was totally not something I should have been doing, ogling my trainer like that, but it was helping me stay focused in some really twisted way. Noah was not the kind of guy I could ever see myself with, not like your Average-Joe kind of hunk like Sean, but there was no harm in a fantasy, was there? Not if it helped me stay motivated.

Fifteen. And all too soon, my eye candy party was over.

"Okay, ladies, take five minutes," Noah clapped once as we finished. "Nice job."

"A break?" Claire snapped, wiping the sweat from her forehead with the back of her hand. "Tom doesn't give us breaks."

"With all due respect, Tom's not your trainer today." Although Noah delivered the words with a smile, they felt no less lethal. "I like to do my workouts a little differently, if that's all right with you."

I nodded to him, a little embarrassed by Claire's behavior. As soon as Noah was out of earshot, I rounded on her.

"What the heck was that?"

"What?" She scowled at me, tossing my towel at my head.

"Hey!" I grabbed it just before it hit my face. "What is your problem today?"

"Nothing. Can't a girl be in a bad mood for once?" She unscrewed the cap of her water bottle and downed half of it in one gulp. I glared at her, hands on my hips, until she was finished.

"You're never in a bad mood, Claire. Not unless something is bothering you."

"So, something's bothering me. What difference does it make to you?" Claire snapping at you is a lot like one of those box turtles that live around ponds in the New England area. Once, on our way home, my mother got out of the car to help a little one cross the road without getting hit by a car. As thanks, it tried to take her pinky finger off. That was the first time I ever heard the expression, "No good deed goes unpunished, girls."

I spotted Noah heading back toward us, so I had to at least get the snapping to cease for the rest of our workout.

"Listen, Groucho Marx," I told her, imitating her firm and commanding authoritative voice as best as I could manage. "Just be nice to Noah for the rest of the session and we'll talk about this later."

"Fine." She almost spit the word at me, but I let it go, turning to Noah instead for our next instructions. He had peeled off his sweatshirt while he was gone, leaving more of himself open for ogling. The rest of my workout was a breeze.

I dragged Claire out for coffee after we finished working with Noah. Not wanting to risk her driving off if we got into our separate cars, I wound my arm through hers and marched straight across the street to this little diner we'd never been to. It was rundown, but clean, and we chose the booth with the least amount of wear and tear for our heart-to-heart sister time. A waitress, who looked like she'd just stepped out of the cab of a tractor trailer, took our order for two cups of coffee, and shuffled off to pour them. As soon as the java had hit the table, I allowed Claire no additional time to stall. I wouldn't let her deny me the information I needed to put the pieces together any longer.

"What's going on with you and Tom?"

With the mug halfway to her lips, Claire froze, her mouth agape. I waited for her to respond, but instead she snapped her mouth shut and stared at me.

"Come on. I'm your sister, Claire. I know you too well to buy any lie you're going to try to sell me." I paused, but still she wouldn't budge. "I noticed something was up the first time you brought me there. You two were practically having sex with your eyes the entire time."

She moved her coffee cup back to the table, spilling a little bit over the rim. Still she wouldn't speak, just kept her eyes on me and her mouth firmly closed.

"You totally slept with him, didn't you?"

"Jen!"

"A-ha! I knew I could get you to talk!" I grinned and took a sip of my own coffee—black with no sugar and, consequently, no calories—to celebrate my success. "So did you do it or not?"

"I'm not going to talk about this with you in some diner, okay?" Even as she was half-heartedly trying to skirt the issue, I could see her cheeks reddening.

"Ooh, Claire!" I poked her in the arm a few times, and then whispered a little chant. "You did your trainer! You did your trainer!"

"Cut it out!" She batted my hand away before raising her mug to her lips to drink her first sip of coffee. Mostly, I think she just wanted to hide behind something for a few seconds.

"All right, fine," I said, sobering my tone a little. "But you have to tell me all the juicy details. And then we'll talk about what the heck was up your butt today."

"I don't like that Noah guy, Jen," she said, coming out from behind her mug to catch my eye. "He looks at you weird."

"I look at him weird," I shrugged. It was true; no point trying to hide it from my sister. Maybe if I led by example, she'd show me the same courtesy. "He's just a trainer, anyway. I'm not interested in him. And he makes me work hard. I like that."

"I just don't think we should workout with him anymore, okay?"

"Why, so we can work out with your lover boy?" I teased.

She delivered her death stare with surprising acuteness for someone so flushed.

"Oh please. It's just a workout," I said. Her burst of laughter caught me off guard. I straightened up in my seat and caught her eye. "What do you think is going to happen, anyway?"

Claire's eyebrows went up. "Seriously?"

"What? Like I'm going to go sleep with him in the locker room after my workout for the day, burn some extra calories?" I started to laugh it off, until I noticed the shift in Claire's expression. The red cheeks were back, her gaze had zoomed elsewhere, and she was biting her bottom lip.

"Shut. Up. You did *not* do that... Did you?" I had to force myself not to yell out the words in the middle of the nearly empty diner. To express my total exasperation, I slapped her hand.

"Ouch!" Claire kept her eyes on the table, rubbing the back of her hand. "I... may have."

CHAPTER EIGHT

"Oh, Claire," I shook my head, sliding back against my seat cushion. "That is so freaking awesome."

"So glad you approve..." she droned, rolling her eyes. My sister's habit of sliding into 'sarcastic teenager' mode when embarrassed had not changed since high school. It drives my mother absolutely crazy, while I have learned how to remain impervious.

"I mean, he's really hot. And he seems like the kind of guy who—"

Claire shot up straight in her seat, her eyes locked in on my own. "Who *what*?"

"Um..." I fidgeted with my napkin for a moment, trying to think of a cover. I'd been about to say 'the kind of guy who only sleeps with really hot chicks.' But given my sister's reaction, I could see that this thin ice needed careful navigation, lest I crack through it and drown. She was always a bit touchy about the guys she hooked up with, but even more so about how her looks influenced them to reciprocate an interest.

When I didn't answer, she just folded her arms across her chest. I noticed she wasn't touching her coffee, that one solitary sip having been enough caffeine to fire up her adrenaline—or so it seemed. It was cooling off, forgotten on the end of the red Formica table top, right next to my empty mug.

"I was going to say," I stalled, making my peace offering with a pleasant smile. "That he seems like a really nice guy, when you get to know him."

"Oh?"

"Come on, Claire. Cut me some slack here. I'm on Team Claire & Tom, okay?" As I spoke the words, her arms lowered, coming to rest on the table. They were still crossed in front of her, more loosely so, but it was not as defensive a posture this way. "I just want the juicy details."

One corner of Claire's mouth twitched upward and I knew I'd hit pay dirt. Story time!

"If you really must know," she began in a raised whisper, leaning over her crossed arms toward me. My eyes were riveted to hers, my lips snapped tightly shut so as not to interrupt what would no doubt be the best story I'd heard in a long, *long* time. I'd been vicariously living through Claire's social life since the end of my undergraduate years and thus, my social life. Unfortunately, she'd been claiming to be in a dry spell for the past few months, so neither one of us was having any fun.

According to Claire, she met Tom through work, where his gym had signed with her marketing agency to do a few TV spots, billboards, and print advertisements in the local newspapers. She'd pitched him a web campaign as well, which he'd loved right from the start, and the two of them hit it off. He invited her down to the gym for some free training sessions as a thank you when the web campaign doubled his business in just six months.

"So it seemed pretty harmless," she continued, reclaiming the cooled mug from the table's edge. The waitress warmed hers up and topped me off with some fresh brew, and we went right back into the story. "I went to work out with him, like, twice a week at the beginning. Eventually, I realized it was such an effective workout, and he was so tuned into what my body needed, that I didn't need to do anything else to maintain my weight and tone. So, I upped my visits to three times. I guess all that time together—*alone*—it just gave us ideas."

Claire stopped talking, stirred some creamer into her coffee, and just stared at me. I blinked at her a couple of times, and still, her mouth stayed shut.

"I'm sorry... I think I fell asleep back there in the middle of your totally lame story."

"You said you wanted details..."

"Claire," I laid my hand on top of her forearm. "That was the version you tell Grandma. I want to know how it *happened*."

"You're not gonna shut up until I tell you something, are you?"

I shook my head.

She sighed. "Okay, fine."

I shifted in my chair, eyes glued to my sister's face, and restrained myself from clapping with glee.

"So, one day, about a month ago, I had to work really late so I pushed back my training session to the last time slot of the day. Tom had me working on the elliptical machine for eight miles or so—"

I groaned, earning a glare from my sister, and waved her on with the story.

"And we ended up working way past when everyone else had already gone home. He's standing there in front of me, watching me work out on the machine, and all of a sudden, our eyes just lock. Like that." She snaps her fingers in front of her face, pulling my focus right to her eyes. "And everything just slows down. I realize I'm not really pushing down on the pedals anymore, just kind of coasting along in slow motion. He leans over the top of the machine..." Claire leaned towards me to demonstrate. "And just plants one on me!"

"No!"

"Yes! Just like that," she smacks the table, spilling more coffee over the rim of her mug. "It's really awkward, by the way, to start passionately kissing someone *around* a piece of exercise equipment."

Mentally, I try to place myself on that treadmill with Noah in front of it. The logistics of trying to make that work—although hot to imagine in great detail—don't make very much sense at all. How would I get my arms around the machine and into that sexy hair? And how on earth would he lift me up and carry me over to the mats? These are the things you have to consider if you're going to start daydreaming about hooking up with your trainer.

"So then what happened?" I have to get more details, overwhelmed by the hypothetical awkwardness that had begun playing itself out in my mind.

"Well, Tom sort of stopped kissing me for a second, made some stupid apology about being so unprofessional. We laughed it off, tried to pull ourselves together…you know, that kind of stuff. But then when he went to hand me my bottle of water, his hand brushed against mine…"

"Uh oh!" I said, maybe a bit too boisterously for the quiet diner. I put a hand over my mouth and tried to shrink lower in my seat. The trucker waitress glowered over at us, looking around for whatever accident she expected I had just caused. Unable to see anything amiss, she turned back to her work.

"And that's how it happened." Claire said abruptly.

"Oh, no! Nuh-uh!"

She shrugged. "What else do you want? Next thing I know, we're on the mats all tangled up, arms and legs, sweaty… And that's that."

I considered the drive-by account of what I usually call 'the fun part' and decided I would need a clearer mental image, when I recast Noah and me in the starring roles. "Were there any oranges close by?"

"What?"

Oh, right. That wasn't supposed to be said out loud. "Never mind."

"Well, there's nothing more to tell, Jen. We did it that one time, then basically, after every workout until three weeks ago."

"When you started bringing me in with you," I finished the thought, my voice deflated. What a terrible sister I was, sabotaging Claire's love life like that. But what a wonderful sister *she* was, sacrificing her precious booty-call times to help me get in shape. I felt a tear coming on; I was so touched by her at that moment.

"Yeah, but that's not why," she offered, trying to sound as committed to her statement as possible. "*You,* we could work around but… I think there's something going on with him. Something at home, or with his family, or… I don't know. He's been acting weird, Jen, and it can't possibly just be because I started working out with you too."

"Are you sure? If I'm in the way, I can try to figure out something else for myself…"

She reached across the table and lightly slapped my arm. "Stop it right now. I'm here to help *you*, not get laid routinely by some hot trainer. While that's nice too, I'm your sister first. If I'm supposed to be with Tom, we'll work it out somehow. And *you* won't be involved, okay?"

"You girls don't tell your mother anything anymore, do you?" says my mom, sighing as she slides back into the couch cushions. "I had no idea about half of these things you're telling me. How have I not heard of any of these guys?"

"Aww, mom…" I answer, feeling a little bit guilty. "You're right. We probably should talk to you more. Maybe we could have avoided half of this mess that way."

"Here I am, sitting around, waiting for you girls to bring your problems to me…" Her voice trails off for a moment, and then she straightens up. "Should I just get better at eavesdropping?"

I want to laugh, but I also don't want to accidentally encourage her. "Why don't we just say that I'll make more of an effort to keep you up to speed, okay?"

"All right," she resigns, skeptically. "But if you don't…"

"Eavesdrop away, Mom."

She grins, reaching one arm around my shoulders to pull me in for a hug. I give myself a moment to catch my breath and collect my thoughts.

"I do remember Sean, though," she says suddenly, stroking my hair gently. "Why didn't you tell me he was back?"

Against my will, a lump forms in my throat. How is it that moms can make this happen so easily? I struggle to swallow it or just talk around it. "I don't know… I didn't want to relive all of that."

"I know, sweetheart," she says, still smoothing my hair down my back. "I know he really hurt your feelings, but if you were thinking of reconnecting with him…"

"I *did* reconnect with him…" I blurt out, feeling that lump tighten. "I didn't think it could happen again, okay? I wanted it to be different this time. I hoped he forgot about that."

"So what happened this time?" she says, not impatiently. I can tell she wants to know everything, to protect me from what she can, to maybe help me see things differently. But at the end of the day, history has repeated itself all over again… "Tell me the rest of the story, Jennifer, and we'll figure this out together."

Taking a deep breath, I decided to keep going. At this point, what else did I have left to lose?

CHAPTER NINE

I didn't want to talk about Sean anymore, now that all of these emotions were springing back to the surface, but I couldn't move the story forward for Mom without revisiting those back-and-forth messages.

Just by clicking that simple *Like* button on one of his photos, I had indeed reignited his interest. I may not have had a clue about what I was doing, but my powers of sociological observation had been treating me well, even out of my depth here on the internet. Within another day or two, he'd *Liked* a few of Olivia's status updates and posted a "Hey, how's it going?" note on my wall. I could tell he was trying to keep me at arm's length, just in case I was toying with him.

Me toying with *him*? The idea was absurd, of course. But then again, looking at Olivia's smoking' hot profile picture, she just might be the type. I could see Sean wanting to take it easy and not seem too eager. I wasn't the hunter here, I was the prey. But in a completely different way than I usually thought of myself as being prey.

Weird.

Anyway, I welcomed his subtle and slow advances, posting replies when he commented, and taking a few moments here and there to visit his profile. In reality, I was all but virtually stalking him, but I didn't leave much evidence of this on his Wall. Instead, I just monitored where he was, what he was up to, who was popping up in his photos, and things like that. Totally normal internet behavior, from what I've learned by watching others interact on Facebook.

Then one day, an amazing thing happened. I was just sitting there, cruising through my usual clicking routine on my profile, then Olivia's, when a new message from Sean appeared in my inbox. My fingers twitched with excitement as I moved the mouse to click it open.

Dear Olivia,

I'm really glad we've had a chance to get back in touch. I remember how much I enjoyed your company back in school, something I didn't know how much I'd missed until now. I hope we can stay friends and maybe even meet up in person sometime.

I'm hosting a party in a couple of weeks, if you'd like to come. There will be lots of people there from school, too, so it might be a nice sort of reunion for you. And we could maybe talk somewhere together, if you like.

Let me know and I'll send you the info.

Sean

I had to fight to stay seated on my chair as I read his note a second and third time. This could be it, my chance to meet him in person and wow him once and for all. Sean O'Dwyer, *the* Sean O'Dwyer who I'd first fallen in love with at the ripe old age of 12. My dream guy, inviting me to a party. To *talk somewhere together* maybe, if I played my cards right.

Immediately, I bolted up from my seat and into the bathroom, where I took a long, hard look at myself in the mirror. Jennifer Smith, staring back at me, did not look as much like Olivia Saunders as I'd been hoping. But there was potential here, I figured, pinning my hair back on top of my head into a bun and sucking in my cheeks. I studied myself from the right and left angles, turned sideways to see the full impact of the 18 pounds I still had left to lose. I was getting closer, but I wasn't there yet. I watched my face fall as the realization sunk in.

There was no way Sean would buy it if I said I was Olivia Saunders, exotic world traveler and successful model/actress. Not like this. Not without seriously kicking some butt in the gym...

I looked down at the rest of my body. And maybe a mani/pedi treatment might be in order too.

On impulse, I ran back to my laptop and typed a quick response to Sean: "Sounds great! I'm in town that weekend, so send me the details and I'll see you there!"

Before I could change my mind, I clicked send and watched it post, becoming a permanent record of the internet. I couldn't take it back now. There was nothing left to do but get to work. I had about fifteen days to get as close as possible to some insane, imaginary personal standard. But I am Jennifer Smith and I have done amazing things before. The only person in my way was me.

So my new mantra became "look like Olivia." I didn't even allow myself to think about what would happen if I couldn't accomplish my goal. Instead, I burned every calorie and ran every mile with this one thought in mind. And with Tom still away on his 'family business,' whatever that meant, I had Noah to help me get there.

By mid-week, I assumed Claire still hadn't heard from Tom, judging by the ugly scowl on her face most days, but she wouldn't admit that she was worried. I didn't push the issue with her. I found her one afternoon standing in the lounge area of Tom's Workout World with her arms crossed tightly over her hot pink running tank top, almost like she was fighting off a chill.

I didn't want to admit it to her, but I wasn't the least bit disappointed to see Noah, instead of Tom, greeting us once again at the front desk that day. Claire was convinced the screaming made us work harder and, thus, we burned more calories. I, however, was not totally convinced that the extra 10 or so calories were really worth all the mental anguish... even if her theory was true. I'm sorry, but I'll always choose a happy workout over one that makes me want to cry myself to sleep at night.

In any case, that day, it wouldn't have mattered what we thought. Noah was training us, and that was that.

"Come on, grumps," I nudged her with my elbow as we followed Noah to the mats. "Is it really so bad?"

"I guess not," she sighed, unwinding her arms. "I'm just… concerned."

"You haven't heard from him?"

Wordlessly, Claire shook her head.

"Claire…" I let her name linger on the air until she turned to me. If Noah could hear us talking, he didn't let on—which I thought was rather polite of him. "Are you guys—"

"I don't know what we are," she said, her voice strained. She heaved a deep sigh and took a moment to gain control of her vocal chords. "It's the same story every time, Jen. Why do I always attract these kinds of guys?"

I gave her a sympathetic look and squeezed her hand. There wasn't time to get into things right now, since we had arrived at the mats. Noah couldn't as easily pretend not to hear, and it would have been really awkward to just keep talking with him staring at us. I knew that he knew about Claire and Tom, but she didn't. Now was not the time to get into it.

Noah started us out with strength training first and I was surprised how well my body was starting to adapt to our workouts. It was still tough, no doubt about it, but my muscles were responding better. I was getting stronger and I could actually tell it was happening. Maybe Claire or Noah wouldn't see it yet, but I could feel it. I wanted to keep going, to see how far I could go.

Sweating, aching, and exhausted, when it was time for our break, I started to notice a new annoyance. All this activity was making my ears sweaty and, thus, my hearing aids were slipping around. There's nothing worse than perspiring underneath your hearing aids. From what I've been told, it's a lot like wearing ear bud headphones on a super-hot day or during a long work out—just gross and slimy. Claire looked over just as I started to fidget with the right one.

"I thought that might happen eventually," she said, offering me a clean towel. "Why not take them out? You can hear well enough to know what's going on, right? I think you'll be okay."

I stared at her for a moment, struck by the idea. Part of me was horrified. Being in public without my hearing aids, while I looked more 'normal' that way, made me extremely vulnerable. I hated them, but not having them was even worse for me. I found myself staring at people's mouths to lip read—well, more than usual—and I had to ask for repetitions a lot. I really, really hated it. But the rest of me knew I would be so much more comfortable without them sliding around in my ears.

Besides, if I was going to look like Olivia in a few days, I needed to work my butt off with nothing stopping me. As this thought passed across my face, Claire took the decision into her own hands.

"Come on, Noah won't mind," she said, standing up. "I'll let him know so he can make sure you make eye contact before he says something."

Springing up, I grabbed her arm. "No, Claire! Don't tell him."

She laughed, sliding her arm from my grip. "He's a professional, Jen. It'll be fine."

Too shocked to do anything, I watched in frozen horror as Claire walked over to Noah, leaned in toward him, and said something. Of course I couldn't hear it, I never can, but they both looked at me simultaneously. Then Noah nodded to her, smiled at me, and Claire walked away.

"I hate you," I told my beloved sister when she returned.

"You'll be thanking me later." She downed a gulp of water then pulled me up to stand beside her. "Come on, leave the extra pair of ears with your bag and let's hit the treadmill."

I sighed, mulling it over in my head. Worth it? Not worth it? Noah had already been directly informed of my impairment, thanks to Claire, so there wasn't much use in hiding it anymore. And if it was going to make the rest of my workout easier... Fine. The hell with it.

Claire and Noah left me alone to sort out my 'accessories,' neither one saying a word, and then I jumped on the treadmill next to my sister. It was a weird sensation to be in a familiar space for the first time without my "extra ears," like being underwater or covering my ears with my hands. Still, I'd never known anything besides a life of coping with or without my hearing aids, so I adjusted quickly.

We did intervals of walking and running for six miles, side by side, and I don't know how in the hell I did that. Granted, Claire could definitely still run faster, but with my eyes locked on Noah for his every instruction, I found something to keep me going. I wanted to do well, almost like I had something to prove. To Claire? To Noah? Or to myself? Either way, I was running, unencumbered by my hearing aids and my own insecurities, and it felt amazing.

"You looked...really happy today, Jen," said Noah, once the treadmill playtime had ended. Claire had gone to the bathroom, leaving us alone in the front lobby. The smile he gave me renewed the wave of heat passing through me that had just begun to cool down after my workout.

I smiled back, fidgeting with the stubborn zipper of my hoodie.

"You know you don't need them around me, right?" He looked at me intently. "If it's more comfortable without them, I will make sure you hear every word I say."

Looking up at him, we shared a silent moment, our eyes connected. I really believed him. Noah could be trusted—not to treat me special because I had a disability or go easy on me because he felt bad for me. He understood the way I felt about my hearing aids and he wanted to help me work around them.

"Thanks," I said, absentmindedly adjusting the left one. "I appreciate that. More than you know."

"I told you so," Claire said, rejoining us. She turned to me and signed 'You're welcome'—a circular motion over her heart. I smirked at her, shaking my head, and signed 'Thank you.'

Noah laughed lightly, looking between us. "You speak sign language?"

"Yeah, ASL," answered Claire. "Our parents learned and taught us when we got Jen's diagnosis. We used to have Family Signing Night once a week—no talking aloud—just for practice. They wanted Jen to be able to communicate with us no matter what."

"Mostly it just became a way for us to talk about people right in front of them," I laughed.

"Wow," he said, impressed. "I always wanted to learn. I can spell my name…"

And he could, more or less, which he demonstrated clumsily. I bit back my laughter at his adorable attempt. Instead, I spelled mine back for him and then signed that I would teach him to sign.

He blinked a few times. "Sorry…didn't catch anything after the letter J."

"I guess you'll just have to be my trainer more often, so you can pick up some signs," I teased.

Claire signed to me: "I bet he's picking one up right now, you flirt." Her eyes scolded me as her hands flew through the words.

"Totally lost," Noah said, shaking his head. "But I'm looking forward to my lessons."

He winked at me and I really wanted to stay and start those lessons right away. If Claire hadn't dragged me away, I probably wouldn't have left.

On the ride home, I finally worked up the nerve to ask Claire about the party.

"And why do you want me to go with you?" she asked, almost offended that I would ask her. "You're a big girl; can't you manage a social evening on your own?"

"Well, it's not that so much as I just want some moral support…" I said, tiptoeing around the important information. I was afraid if she knew the party was Sean's, she wouldn't agree to go. I didn't think I could convince her that things would be different this time. "I really like the guy that's hosting and I was hoping you could just come along… You know, in case…"

As we cruised to a stop at the intersection's red light, Claire turned on me with a look of disbelief. "In case what? You want me to hold the video camera, Jen?"

"No!" I shrieked, feeling my face grow hot. "It's not like that. I meant in case I panic and don't know what to do. I'm not good at parties, Claire. That's not my thing."

"I don't know…"

She was teetering on the edge, just waiting for another gentle nudge. I could sense her pending *yes* and I knew I had to be careful what I said. Moving again, I let Claire drive a few more blocks before I decided to continue with my final desperate plea.

"When was the last time we went out together and did something fun?"

Claire stole a look over at me before shifting her attention back to the road. I could already see her mouth twitching into a reluctant smile. "Okay, okay. I'll go."

Nailed it.

And speaking of nails… "Thanks, Claire! I'll even treat us both to a pedicure beforehand, okay?"

Two birds, one stone. Jennifer Smith is a genius.

CHAPTER TEN

Of course, I couldn't spend all my time running on a treadmill and daydreaming about my first meeting with Sean in over a decade. There were still the matters of my project—you know, the *actual* purpose of Olivia's profile—and my regular classwork. Graduating seemed like such an inconvenience when there were more exciting things to do now.

Luckily, I kept busy enough that my days passed in a blur, featuring many rounds of mindless clicking through Olivia's profile. It was getting me nowhere, and boring me to tears, so I decided one afternoon to make a list of things to intentionally study instead. A plan of action to shake things up a bit. Dr. Chase would've been proud of my commitment. So far, more than two months in, I'd gotten a good handle on how strangers reacted to random friend requests. Looks seemed to factor prominently, given the difference between Olivia's staggering number of acceptances and my own miserable failure to attract a sizable number of "stranger friends." Outside of that, there had to be something else to study, but what?

My friends, obviously.

I decided to tackle the phenomenon of inclusion on the internet, beginning with a log-in to my own profile. I friended Olivia myself, hoping to establish at least one connection to her so that my friends might get her as a friend suggestion. Once a few of them friended her, the rest might follow suit, even though none of them knew her. If they thought they were supposed to, or wanted to, they would friend her just to be included. At least, that was the theory. Time would tell if that worked or not. I decided to jumpstart things by sending a few friend requests from Olivia herself and switched back to her profile to get started.

Through Olivia's profile, I found myself and clicked on my Friends List to see who I wanted to start with. Aside from Claire, my class study partner Lyla, and Dr. Chase, no one knew a thing about this project. It was truly the ideal conditions to conduct a study like this, so I was proud of myself for not having a big mouth. I scrolled through the list, picking a couple of friends from high school that I hadn't seen in a while, and let Olivia send them a request. Maybe they'd think Olivia was another classmate, new to Facebook.

I kept going, trying to find a few from each walk of my life. College, work, random friends through friends. In total, I sent about a dozen requests, jotted down all the names to keep track of their responses, and had nothing to do but wait. Of course, a thirteenth name caught my eye, all the way down at the bottom of my list under W.

Noah Wayland, trainer extraordinaire.

He looked so out of place amidst all my other friends. In fact, he was as out of place on my own friends list as Sean was on Olivia's. The two could've easily swapped places, yet here they were. If this was true, shouldn't I be able to friend them each in turn from my *other* profile?

I was starting to confuse myself with this tangled mess.

Anyway, I clicked on Noah's name and spotted the Request Friendship button up in the top right corner of the screen. I could send one, just like that, and see what he does. Would he think Olivia was my hot roommate? Another sister? She looked enough like me—because she was me, after all—that she could easily be mistaken for a Smith family member. Or would Noah just blindly accept the request based on that smoking hot profile picture?

I took a deep breath, closed my eyes, and clicked it. When it was over, I didn't let myself dwell on it. I couldn't let myself think of this as another social experiment, as a way to test his moral character. After that nice session the other day, and the interest in learning ASL, I really didn't know what to think about him. Using Olivia was a quick and easy way to see if he was like the rest of these guys.

Next, I friended my sister Claire and scrolled through her list of friends for a similar study group. That's how I made the shocking discovery that Claire and Olivia already had one friend in common: Tom Payone.

Staring at his profile, it finally clicked. He was one of the first few guys to have targeted Olivia as a friend before I ever requested it. That's why Tom looked so familiar when I first met him at the gym. What was he doing, trolling the internet for hot girls and sending them friend requests when he was supposed to be in some undefined relationship with my sister? I guess that's the problem with undefined relationships, isn't it? I clicked on "See Friendship" to see what other interactions he and Olivia had been having. I couldn't believe how stupid I'd been, not to connect this Tom with *the* Tom.

But lots of people are named Tom. Anyone could make that mistake.

Facebook spit back a long list of interactions that I'd been ignoring with the usual influx of dirty, disgusting messages from men through Olivia. Ugh. Messages on my wall from Tom, saying "Hey, how are things?" and "How's the family doing?" like we knew each other. Or, rather, like he and Olivia knew each other. Like he was keeping up appearances to make a friendship with her look legitimate. For who's benefit, I didn't know.

More disturbing than that, however, was what I found in my Messages history. There were several inappropriate one-line messages, just like the usual noise I received here, including a personal favorite: "That looks like a nice bra. Can I talk you out of it?"

Seriously, Tom?

His most recent message, sent just before he disappeared for this mysterious "family stuff," was a bit more involved:

Hey Olivia,
Heading out to a party in your area tonight. Want to meet up? I've got something *huge* to show you... big enough to share with a friend if you like. Message back if you want a piece.
XXX - Tom

Cute. Just... adorable. Who was this maniac my sister was *kinda* dating? And why was she even *kinda* dating him? She had to know; I had to tell her what kind of man she was dealing with. Granted, they weren't technically exclusive or anything, so Claire couldn't really claim any kind of wrong-doing in this situation, not over some inappropriate messages online. Single boys will be single boys, right? I guess the most important thing was how he would treat my sister during their relationship, if they ever made things more official.

For now, there wasn't much to do about it. As far as I knew, Tom was long since out of the picture anyway. Why hurt Claire further by telling her about all of this noise too? I kept the messages—just in case—and put it out of my mind.

The day of Sean's party arrived without any fanfare, as I almost hoped it would. Instead, it was a rainy, nasty day in November and I felt like I'd been hit by an 18-wheeler truck. Fighting off a terrible headache and some sinus congestion, I dragged myself from my bed and into the shower. As I plucked, shaved, exfoliated, and moisturized every part of my body, I was starting to feel better. It wasn't the best day ever, but I could still hold out hope that it would end on a high note.

Fully buffed from head to toe, I towel dried my hair and stared at my changing body in the full-length mirror. *We're getting there*, I thought to myself, very proud of how much I'd achieved in just over two months of hard work. My body was starting to shape itself into something more feminine, less... I don't know. Less... blobby? I wasn't a blob, but there were parts of me that just kind of spilled over, you know? They were going away, leaving some disconcerting extra skin behind, but nothing some Spanx couldn't fix.

As I thought of it, I reached for my brand new Spanx—a size smaller than my previous set—and slid them on, reveling in the smoother look of my body beneath them. Yes, this would do nicely. I would look perfect, or as perfect as possible. There was still the matter of 12 annoying pounds to lose, but I could flatten some parts and Miracle-Bra some other parts until I got pretty damn close indeed.

See? Becoming Olivia was just like playing dress up.

I met Claire at our favorite nail place, just down the street from her apartment, and handed her the coffee I'd picked up along the way. It was nice to sit and relax with her again, without any gym appointments to keep or parental obligations to uphold.

"So where is this party tonight, anyway?" she asked, handing over a bottle of violet-hued nail polish to the pedicurist. Claire pointed to a pink bottle on the shelf in front of me. "That one, Jen. It's feminine and sexy. Perfect."

I took her advice, passing the bottle over to the pedicurist waiting for me to climb into the bubbling foot bath. Once settled into the massage chair, coffee at my side, I let myself relax a little bit.

"It's an old friend from school," I shrugged, flipping through the magazine at the top of the pile between our two chairs. It was outdated and faded from too much use, but it was a big improvement from my usual dry reading material for class. "You probably wouldn't remember him. He was in my year."

"Oh, okay," she said, taking a sip of coffee. "So... you like him, huh?"

I tried not to blush, burying my attention deep into the pages of the magazine. "Yeah, I guess. We've been catching up online recently and I'm hoping there's something between us in person."

I stole a quick glance at her and saw she was watching me carefully. I could see it on her face: she thought she was coming with me tonight to help pick up the pieces when this guy—like all the others before him—broke my heart. She didn't believe he was interested in me any more than I did. Why was I even going to this thing?

"Well, I can't wait to meet him," Claire smiled, changing her tactics. "I wonder if I'll recognize him…"

With that, we let the conversation drop and resigned ourselves to reading side by side in silence. Claire laughed a little when the pedicurist scrubbed her feet, but otherwise, made no sound. I was too happy about the massage chair to care much about talking.

All too soon, though, our pampering was over and it was time for me to go home and begin a pointless wrestling match with my wardrobe. Finding something to wear was never easy for me, not even when I had nowhere special to go and no one special to impress. I was totally doomed.

"Um, Claire?" I asked, as we walked back to our cars. "Do you think you could help me pick something to wear?"

If anyone knew what Olivia would wear, it was Claire. Her style was always impeccable, and far superior to my own. I also knew that getting her hands on my wardrobe was another secret wish of my sister's. She responded only too quickly with a *yes*, dragged me through the mall on a dizzying shopping spree, and dropping me squarely into my living room with a stack of apparel and accessories I didn't remember buying.

"Well, that was interesting…" I muttered, sorting through the pile on the couch, not sure where to begin. "So what am I supposed to do now?"

"This is just some basic everyday stuff here, Jen," she said, taking on her authoritative voice. "You'll want to wear these things to class and out shopping and stuff. It was time for you to replace those frumpy clothes you're too small for, anyway…"

She stopped, smiling directly at me.

"That sounds great, doesn't it? *You're too small* for some of your clothes! Look! These are a size Medium, Jen. I'm really proud of you, you know."

I smiled back at her, and realized that the new clothes were worth every penny. She had a point. I couldn't just lose the weight if I wasn't going to dress the part. I didn't need to start baring cleavage, but I could certainly afford to buy clothing in the right size for a change, instead of a size or two bigger to hide my frumpy figure. It felt good to do something for me, for a change.

"So what am I wearing tonight?" I asked, in an effort to get us back on track.

"This," Claire said grandly, sliding a gorgeous black something-or-other out of a Macy's bag. "This is your new LBD."

"LB...what?"

"Little black dress, Jen." She rolled her eyes at me, holding it up in one hand and gesturing with the other. "See? It's little, black, and it's a dress. It's an LBD, a wardrobe necessity. This is what you wear when you want to look sophisticated and attract attention."

"Won't I be a little overdressed?"

"A-ha!" She exclaimed, waving it around in triumph. "That's the beauty of the LBD! You can dress it up or dress it down. If we pair this with the right jewelry and shoes, you'll fit right in."

I squinted at her for a moment, letting her words settle on my fashion-dense brain.

"Just trust me, okay? I've got this. I know what I'm doing."

Then, without my permission, Claire began flying around me in a flurry of activity. She was like my fairy godmother, come to rescue me from my own poor fashion circumstances and dress me for the ball. Makeup got tossed at my face, my hair was wrestled into some form of styling device, and eventually, that LBD made its way onto my body. I had to give Claire credit: whether she believed Sean would give me the time of day or not, she was certainly doing as much as she could to make the night go in my favor. I have the best sister in the world.

CHAPTER ELEVEN

Claire convinced me to let her drive so I could concentrate on staying calm and looking beautiful. Those were her words, not mine. I plugged the address into her GPS and tried to regulate my pulse as she sped along the road, taking turn after turn to bring me closer to Sean's house.

He lived in a quiet part of town, in a large Colonial house at the end of a cul-de-sac—his parents' place, I assumed. Most of the houses around his were darkened, no lights on and no cars in the driveway. His house, on the other hand, was fully lit up. Music filtered out of the closed windows and into the neighborhood, as guest after guest spilled in through the front door. I'd never been to a house party like this before, not even in college, and I really wanted to turn on my heel and bolt in the other direction.

I took one look at Claire, as she pulled over to the curb and parked behind a silver Audi, and could see that she was having the same thought.

"What's the matter?" I asked, trying to sound light and eager.

"We're at the O'Dwyers' house," she said, flatly. After a pause, she turned on me and grabbed my wrist. "Why are we here, Jen?"

I tried to back away from her as much as I could, flattening myself against the passenger side door. I couldn't break Claire's grip around my wrist, though, or her death glare.

"Claire, let go. I told you… we've been talking online. I really wanted to see him again in person… and I…"

"Why do you think this will be any different from the last time, Jen?" Her voice was high-pitched, almost tinged with a hint of panic. "Sean O'Dwyer? Come on!"

"Why is it so crazy that I want to see him? I'm an adult now and so is he. People change; I've changed. Can't I have another chance?" I fought to keep my own panic out of my voice, and probably failed. "Please come in with me. I've worked so hard to be… to be what he expects me to be. I have to try."

"What do you mean, *what he expects you to be*? What have you been telling him, Jen?" She finally let go of my wrist, but only so she could run her hand angrily through her hair. I watched her wrestling to keep her frustration in check, at least long enough to hear me out.

"I may have… friended him as Olivia," I said sheepishly. As Claire turned her glare back on me, I saw that her expression was positively lethal and I was just a little bit terrified. Desperate to get my whole story out before she opened her mouth to say whatever she was thinking, I dove into the most abridged version of events possible. I told her about him recognizing me but being terrible at names, then how we had been flirting back and forth, and I'd been working so hard at the gym so I could look like Olivia.

"There are so many things wrong with this; I don't even know where to begin…" Her acid tone wasn't as bad as it could have been, so it was a small victory. "He thinks your name is Olivia?"

"Yes, but I was planning on telling him it was my fake model name or something," I said, waving it off. "I was going to figure that out later. What I really need is for him to see me and think it's the same person. I tried so hard to…"

"And you brought *me* with you to do this?"

"You're my sister, Claire... I wanted the moral support." I felt helpless, like I was losing the battle. I hadn't come all this way for her to drop me off on the porch and speed away into the night.

"Fine, I'm here." She said, throwing open the car door. "Let's go and get this over with. I'll be your moral support. I'll gladly play my part in this fool-proof scheme you've concocted. But when it doesn't work, Jen..."

Climbing out of my side of the car, I bit down hard on my lip to collect my nerves. I couldn't let her words or her anger shake my confidence now. I'd known this would happen when Claire discovered it was Sean's party. I'd prepared myself for her to freak out and get overprotective. Now, all I could do was go in there and face him for myself.

She trailed a little bit behind me as I pushed my way into the crowded living room, like she was my bodyguard or something. I resigned myself to accept Claire's attitude and carry on with the plan. First, I had to find Sean for myself.

He's been right about one thing: there were definitely people there that I recognized from school. Not anyone that I really wanted to see, of course, mostly the other jocks and popular kids who'd made my life miserable as a junior high and high school student. I fought the urge to slink around them and instead strode confidently through the crowd, nudging a former quarterback here and an ex-cheerleader there. They weren't the reason I was here; I couldn't let them distract me.

And then, I saw him. There he was, Sean O'Dwyer, in all his handsome glory. He was standing in a mixed group of guys and girls in the kitchen, telling a story about some legendary baseball game he pitched back in the day, and I found myself instantly captivated by his voice. It hadn't changed at all, still ringing out with that powerful timber, that hint of pure cheerfulness. I listened to him talk, frozen in place long enough for Claire to catch up to me, and fell enraptured by a story I'd heard before. No, a story I'd witnessed firsthand, actually. I never missed a single one of Sean's baseball games in high school, so of course I knew it well.

"I'm three outs from throwing my first no-hitter, the last game of the regular season, and this huge power-hitting kid comes up to the plate. It was Bobby Jordan from, uh, Brighton High? Right? Remember him?" He smiled at his own memories, talking louder and louder to work the crowd up for the story's big finale. For a moment, if I closed my eyes, it was like nothing in my life had ever changed. There was Sean, just feet away from me, and here I was, unnoticed and unseen.

Just as I opened my eyes again, ready for Sean to keep talking, I realized he'd stopped mid-sentence and was staring at me.

"Olivia?" He almost whispered it, nearly too quiet for me to hear. If I hadn't been staring at his mouth, I might not have known what he said.

This was it. This was my moment, the one I'd dreamt of for weeks, months. Okay, for years. Sean, *the* Sean, was walking directly toward me, pushing other people out of the way to get closer. As he approached, I could smell his cologne—mixed with the scent of beer—waft towards me. I had done it. I had finally...

"Olivia, hi," he said at last. But he wasn't talking to me.

"Um..." said Claire, at a total loss. She grabbed my arm, her eyes darting from Sean's face to mine. There was a silent plea in those eyes, asking me what she should do. I didn't know what to tell her. I still couldn't believe what I was hearing.

"I'm so glad you can make it," Sean said, grinning ear to ear. He was totally smitten with Claire, the one he thought was Olivia. How could he think it was her? Olivia was me... she was a picture of *me*, just doctored to look a little thinner and a little...

Oh my God.

I looked at my sister as though for the first time, noting the shape of her face, the wave of her blonde hair, the contour of her shoulders, her waist. I'd made myself into Claire with all of those photo edits. *Claire* was *Olivia*, at least in body. How could I not see this before?

As the silence between Sean and Claire continued, they both seemed to look to me for answers. As my eyes connected with Sean's, I knew that there was still hope for me somehow. There was still a way for me to win Sean, once and for all. I'd come too far to give up now.

"Hi Sean," I said, smiling easily. "It's Jennifer. We went to school together too... and I'm Olivia's roommate." I nudged Claire as I said this, and she turned on me with a look of sheer terror. Or anger. Something unpleasant.

"Hi," she said timidly. "Um, Sean. Nice to see you."

When Sean leaned over and hugged my sister, it really only stung a little. Just the tiniest bit.

But this, like all things, was only temporary.

Back at home, I unfolded the rest of my plan for my sister. Bringing Claire along had seemed like a disaster at first, but now I could see it for what it really was: the perfect solution to all my problems. If Sean thought Claire was Olivia and I was her roommate, then found out that Olivia was a heartless bitch who would mistreat him and lead him on... that left me, plain old Jennifer, to rush in and save the day. It was the perfect plan, if only I could get Claire to agree to play her part in the charade.

"No, no, no," she shook her head vehemently, almost hard enough to produce sound. I was worried for her neck. What if she just snapped it right in half, shaking so hard?

"Please," I squeezed my hands together in a prayer, leaning forward toward her on the couch. "This is the only way, Claire."

"So just because I'm *slightly* thinner and have the right hair color, you think I can pull off acting like some imaginary person you've created?"

"You also have bigger boobs," I said pointedly. "But Victoria, her Secret, and I are working on that. Besides, it's just for one night, just long enough to do this one thing... please?"

She shook her head again, but more softly this time. If she was starting to resist less, that could be a good sign for me. Keep it up and Operation: Olivia Implosion would be a success.

"I'm sorry, Jen, but I don't think it's a good idea. Just cut ties with Sean once and for all and forget about it. Nothing good ever comes from making up lie after lie to get close to someone.

Either tell him the truth and get it over with, or just end the project early. I'm sure you have enough data to write your paper."

I couldn't bring myself to tell Claire that I'd already started writing the paper based on what I'd learned with Olivia's profile so far. She was right; I had more than enough material to write all 20 pages and delete the profile, but I found that I couldn't. Was I addicted to the freedom of anonymity? To being someone I wasn't? Was it Sean that was keeping me online? Without the profile, I'd have no tie to him at all. And then what?

"If you really won't help me..." Before I could finish my sentence, Claire was shaking her head again. I sighed deeply and leaned back against the arm of the couch. "I'll just have to come up with something else. Do you think I could pay a stripper to do it for me?"

Claire smacked me in the face with a pillow.

"Well, if my sister—who's already been mistaken for Olivia—won't help me, what choice do I have but to turn to prostitutes?"

Another smack in the face.

"Okay, okay! Stop!" I laughed, taking a third hit to the side of my temple. "I'll fix it on my own. I promise! No strippers or hookers."

I took one final blow before Claire started laughing herself, then I wrestled the pillow from her grip and hit her back a few times.

CHAPTER TWELVE

A few days later, Tom was back from his little vacation, the Smith sisters were back in action with their original trainer at the gym, and I'd lost Claire's attention for good. With Tom in the way, there was no hope of me convincing her to help me with Sean. I'd have to think of something else.

Now that we were back in Tom's line of fire, I realized how little I'd really missed his kamikaze training approach. His vein bulged and his spittle flew about me as I did some burpees that night, sending a fiery burn right up the muscles of my arms into my shoulders. I kept hoping that Tom would walk behind me just as I was lunging backwards, kicking out my legs, but it never happened.

What did happen, however, shook things up in a way I didn't expect at all.

"Ouch!" Claire yelped, collapsing onto her mat. "Oh no. Ow, ow, owwwww."

She cradled her ankle with two hands, rocking against the pain. Tom was by her side in a split second, leaving me mid-countdown. I didn't have a problem with that, since I'd already stopped doing the reps anyway.

"What happened, Claire?" I said meekly, wanting to help her but not sure how. Tom seemed to be taking care of it, though, by stretching out her leg and tenderly inspecting the injured ankle.

"I'm fine," she answered. Tom turned her ankle over in his hand. "Just...ouch!"

"I don't think it's broken," he said, sitting back on heels. "But we should probably get you an x-ray to be sure. It's better not to take any chances with a joint injury."

Still on the mat, I watched Tom play efficient nursemaid to my sister. With the ice pack and bandage Noah brought over, Tom had Claire's ankle padded and cooling down in no time. Then he swung her up into his arms, called out some orders to the other trainers, and started heading toward the door.

"I'll call you, Jen," my sister yelled out to me. "Don't worry about me."

And then she was gone, literally swept off her feet by her trainer.

It all happened so quickly that, when it was over, the room felt oddly quiet. Noah, sitting on the mat next to me, was the first to speak.

"He didn't waste any time, did he?" He almost added a chuckle, but my sharp look cut him off.

"She could be really hurt, Noah."

"No, that's not what I—" His face fell. "You're right. Sorry, I've just never seen Tom move so fast."

The idea that Tom would be so concerned, not because one of his patrons was injured but because it was *Claire*, cheered me a bit. I knew how Claire felt about him, more or less, but it was nice to see that the object of her affection returned some of those feelings. I offered Noah a smile as thanks.

"He's not like that with any of the other clients?"

"Well, he's a careful guy, pretty attentive. And he generally doesn't mess around with injuries," Noah said, thinking. He stretched his legs out in front of him, the toes of his sneakers touching. "But I can't say I've ever seen him carry someone out the door. He usually just calls the ambulance."

We laughed about this for a moment, and the almost frantic reaction Tom had to something as commonplace as a sprained ankle. I mean, I hoped Claire would be okay, but the whole incident had been a bit comical in its severity.

"Hey," Noah straightened up suddenly, struck by an idea. "What are you doing right now?"

I looked down at myself, still clad in my sweaty gym shorts and a loose-fitting t-shirt, sitting cross-legged on a mat in the middle of an empty gym. I needed a shower, badly, and I wasn't even sure I'd packed my deodorant in my gym bag today.

"Why?" I was a bit hesitant to go anywhere, especially with Noah, looking like this.

"What if we take the rest of your workout on the road?" he shrugged. "I'm off the clock and I need to get my own workout in, but this is the last place I want to hang out after I've been working all day. Want to go for a run?"

He stood up, offering a hand to help me to my feet. I took it, but stayed sitting for a moment, considering the myriad excuses I could make to get out of this.

"Running?" I stalled, pushing off the mat while Noah pulled me up. "Like, *off* the treadmill?"

He feigned a look of shock, leaning back. "Jennifer Smith, if you've never gone for a run outside, I feel genuinely sorry for you."

"That's not nice," I said, hands on my hips. "Can you please try to remember that I'm new to all of this and cut me some slack?"

"As your interim trainer, I will do no such thing. Come on, you can leave your stuff here, we'll pick it up on the way back." With that, he was jogging toward the door, leaving the empty gym to the other two trainers, and waving for me to follow him. "Let's go, Lazy."

With one last look of lament for my comfortable square of padded gym mat, I decided it's not every day that you get permission to chase after a hot man in public. And outdoors, no less. So I threw caution to the wind, quite literally, and sprinted toward the door.

"That's more like it," he said, winking at me. And as soon as the door opened, he took off.

Noah ran like he was born to do it, every one of his muscles working together in a choreographed motion. Like a cheetah hunting its prey, his every movement was graceful and smooth. Despite running behind him, I felt like I might be best portrayed as the escaping prey, clunky in my attempts to keep up. I stumbled over a few rocks or tree roots here and there, the debris of the sidewalk proving to be an unforeseen challenge of running outside instead of on a treadmill.

A nice and safe treadmill, stored indoors without any natural interference like weather or falling leaves.

The day was brisk, since it was early November, but between my previous workout at the gym and the exertion of the run itself, I didn't feel the cold after a few minutes. Noah was still running up ahead of me, only a couple hundred feet or so, but I couldn't tell if I was catching up or if he was letting me. Determined to make up the difference, I dug deeper to pull out that last bit of whatever it was that motivated me when I was near Noah. I found it, and the result was a sudden push forward. Within a few moments, we were finally side by side, our legs working in sync. He actually grinned to see me running next to him.

"Welcome to the front of the pack," he said, barely fighting for breath.

I couldn't answer, I was so winded. Instead of waiting for a response, he stepped up his own pace a notch, leaving me behind again. So this is the game, I thought to myself. Cat and mouse.

He darted around the corner, headed toward Boston Common, and I followed as closely as my throbbing muscles would allow. My thighs burned, my arms ached, and my stomach was growling. Audibly, I was sure of it. But there was Noah, up ahead of me, running like some jungle cat set loose on the city streets. I couldn't let him get away from me and I had no idea why it mattered so much, just that it did.

I checked my energy reserves again, seeing if there was anything else to come up with. Scraping the bottom of the fuel tank, I found one last burst and let it propel me forward, closing the gap between us. I leapt over the curb as we crossed the street, closer and closer to him. Just as we crossed the gateway into the Common, I caught up again.

"Ooh, kitty has claws, doesn't she?" He chuckled and I couldn't tell if he was mocking me.

I wanted to laugh with him, but there wasn't any oxygen left in my lungs. Seeing the pained look of struggle contorting my features, Noah mercifully slowed things down. He always seemed to know exactly when I needed some time to recover. He eased our pace to a light jog, enough to keep my heart rate elevated while letting my lungs get reacquainted with air.

"Thanks," I said, managing a weak smile. "For the break."

"Don't get too comfortable here," he warned playfully. "You never know when I'll take off again."

"Yes, I do," I smirked. "You'll only take off again when you're confident I can catch you."

"A full sentence? You're speaking in sentences, now? I think that means you can catch me."

And then, once again, Noah took off across Boston Common, leaving me in his dust. My arms and legs had just gotten used to the slowed pace, the aching in my lungs had just started to dissipate. I wasn't ready for this yet, but somehow, because Noah believed I was, I found something inside to push myself forward.

I started going faster and faster, darting around a stroller here or there, hearing the thumps of my feet on the pavement. As I let my mind finally process everything that was around me, I realized how much more exciting it was to run outside, with so much to see and hear, people to pass by, nature to enjoy. The cool air was another bonus, wicking the sweat from my forehead as it swept by me. Noah was right to get me out of the gym, out of my comfort zone, and give me something to really push for. At that thought, I noticed he was almost near enough to reach out and grab his t-shirt, so I looked down at my feet and silently pleaded with them to keep moving.

When I looked up again, it was too late to do anything. Another body was mere inches from colliding with mine, someone walking or running toward me along the pathway. I'd drifted in front of him, while I was talking to my shoes, and we crashed into each other. On impact, one of my hearing aids popped out and bounced over the sidewalk. The rest of me crashed to the pavement in a tangled heap of limbs, and my skin stung in several places, scratched up on rocks and other natural debris.

Just when I thought treadmills were for losers.

Disoriented, I tried to absorb what had happened, and see who I'd hit. It was a young guy, around my own age, wearing a baseball cap and sweats. He must've been out for his own run across the Common when I'd so unkindly cut him down.

"I'm really sorry," I stumbled over the words, shamed beyond reason. My face burned with the effort. "I should watch where I'm going."

"Me too," he said, climbing to his feet. He wasn't too tall, a little shorter than Noah, but he had a nice, trim build. A daily run was probably part of his regular maintenance, just like Claire. The thought made me feel like a total hack, out here running, disturbing the good-doing athletic citizens of the world by crashing into them mid-stride. "Are you okay?"

I'd know what voice anywhere.

I managed a nod, swallowing the embarrassment and anxiety threatening to spew forth from my mouth. I kept my lips closed against the words and concentrated instead on standing back up. I shook out my legs, finding them in perfect working order, although a bit scratched up. I felt okay to keep moving, so I looked at my victim to tell him as much, but my voice froze up instead.

Because staring at me from underneath that baseball cap, was a face I'd spent a lot of time hovering cursors over on my computer. A face that had broken my heart once before and almost did so again this past Saturday night.

"Sean?" The name was out of my mouth before I even knew I was thinking it. Immediately, I slapped my hand against my naked ear, praying he hadn't noticed my runaway "accessory." Where was that thing anyway?

His eyebrows furrowed as he considered me, all sweaty and disgusting, standing before him.

"Do I know you?" He blinked a few times. "I'm sorry if I don't remember. I'm terrible with names."

"Well, we've sort of met…" I stopped, not sure how to take the news that he could forget me in four days' time. "This weekend?"

"Oh…" His voice trailed off and he started looking past me, like he just needed an excuse and he'd be off running again. In hindsight, I should've just let him leave, rather than complicate things any further.

"I'm… um… I'm…" A total idiot? Totally screwed? A gigantic liar? Might as well go all the way, if I'd made it this far already. "Olivia Saunders is… um…"

"You know Olivia?" His whole persona changed at the mention of her name, just like that. Sean's smile brightened, no longer just a result of faked politeness, and his attention refocused on me. I felt like I was onstage in that instant, performing a careful ballet for a rabid audience just waiting to tear me apart at the first misstep.

"I'm…" Exactly how was I supposed to explain my sociology project in a not-boring way that made me not the bad guy? I guess if I didn't care what Sean thought about me, it would've been much easier to do. But then again, would I even feel the need to explain it at all? Would I have pretended I didn't recognize him, like any normal human being?

So no, thanks to my weird moral hang-ups, I couldn't blow my cover and hurt his feelings. I wouldn't admit right then and there that I was Olivia, a scheming liar toying with others' emotions just to get a better grade and earn my Master's degree with honors. I needed to keep up the ruse, just for now. Until I had a better plan.

"I'm Olivia's roommate. Remember me? From the party?"

"Oh, right! Nice to see you again," he grinned again, shaking my hand. Then, just as abruptly, his eyes were searching in every direction around me. "Is Olivia with you?"

"Uh...no. She's out of town." The answer fell on my tongue easily and I knew then what I had to do. If I kept Olivia out of the way long enough, maybe I could keep Sean's attention for myself. "So, uh... how have you been? You know, since school? We didn't really get a chance to catch up at the party, so..."

"I'm not sure if I remember you from school," Sean said, puzzled. "What was your name again?"

"Hey Jen, what happened?" Noah cruised to a halt in front of me just then, almost toe to toe with Sean. "Sorry. Who's this?"

"Just an old classmate I ran into. Literally," I answered him, wincing. "Sean, this is my trainer Noah. And Noah, this is Sean, a former schoolmate and a pal of my roommate."

A moment passed between them, something I didn't really understand, but a lot like they were sizing each other up. Guys.

"Nice to meet you, Jen," Sean said suddenly. "Could you tell Olivia I said hello? I hope she's back in town soon so we can hang out. If she ever takes a break from those modeling shoots, that is. Anyway, take care!"

As Sean jogged away from us, Noah's eyes looked to me for some answers. A roommate who was a model had no doubt piqued his interest. Next thing I knew, he'd be asking me to bring her around to the gym sometime, or inviting himself back to my place for private sessions—just so he could meet her accidentally. You know, all in the line of duty.

"Yeah, I know, I have a..." I started to explain, distracted by the search for my missing hearing aid. Noah spotted it first, pointing it out in a patch of dandelions. I snatched it up, only slightly mortified. "What was I saying? Oh! Olivia! Yeah, I have a—"

"A huge gushing wound on your knee," Noah cut in, alarm in his voice. "Let's get you fixed up, okay? Come on. Back to the gym with you. To the first aid kit!"

CHAPTER THIRTEEN

So maybe my wound wasn't huge or gushing, but Noah certainly treated it like it was the most serious injury ever sustained on his watch. Maybe it was... Still, the irony of his overreaction to my skinned knee after making fun of Tom wasn't lost on me.

For a big, muscly guy, Noah had surprisingly gentle hands. Not that I can say I've been tended to by someone like him before, or even any guy, for that matter. But it surprised me nonetheless. Back at the gym, I watched—mesmerized—as he cleaned and bandaged my scraped knee. With the gym's first aid kit at the ready, he swabbed my entire knee with antiseptic, being sure to pick out the tiny bits of gravel as he did so. I winced at each twinge, looking at the raw, red skin around the scrape.

"It doesn't look too bad," he said, studying it. With his hands all over my leg and his face just inches from my skin, I have never been so glad to have shaved in the morning.

He rifled around in the kit for a tube of Neosporin, which he applied liberally, and then for the bandages. A scraped knee was no big deal, something every kid gets pretty regularly. But as a grown woman, watching a grown man—no, watching *Noah*—kneel at my feet and tend to it so... tenderly... It was disproportionately intense.

"Does it hurt much?" he asked, admiring his handiwork. He was careful to smooth down each corner of the bandage completely, so it wouldn't peel up and stick to my clothes. I hate when that happens and then they're all linty and won't stick to anything else. It's like Noah knew this.

"Not too bad," I said, then caught his skeptical look. "Well, not anymore."

"I think you'll pull through," he teased, the corner of his mouth twitched. Slowly, he rose from his position on the floor and as his lips passed mine, I felt myself lean towards them. Like they were magnetic or something.

Noah noticed and it stopped him in his tracks, half-sitting in the seat next to me. As he hovered there, a million thoughts zoomed through my brain, most of them negative in nature and none of them totally coherent. The word "stupid" featured prominently. So I did what any normal girl would do under the circumstances to compensate: I giggled. And then, I wanted to slap myself again.

Instead, I cut my giggling short, almost mid-breath. For a moment, the air thickened with silence. I felt like my hearing aids should be buzzing from the increasing pressure around my head. We just sat there, breathing in that air and staring at each other.

Noah cracked first, erupting into laughter. He had a full, hearty laugh—one I could've heard even without my accessories in place from across a crowded mall. The kind of laugh that goes viral.

And so I laughed along with him, out of both my relief and the delight he inspired with that sound. Together, we laughed for several minutes without trying to stop or to speak. I'm not truly sure what we were laughing about, but I couldn't stop myself. I hadn't laughed like that since... I couldn't even tell you, it had been so long.

Eventually, as do all good things, our chuckles came to an end. The laughter subsided into short bursts and quiet shakes. I wiped a stray tear from the corner of my eye and tried to relax my facial muscles, aching from the exertion. I'd laughed so hard, it actually hurt.

Noah's laughs stopped abruptly and the sudden lack of sound drew my eyes to his face. His expression had shifted somehow, from out-of-control laughter to deep thoughtfulness, like he was about to say something profound. My face fell as I studied him, studying me.

Before I knew what was happening, he leaned in and kissed me. The kind of kiss that makes your heart stop beating for a minute. His lips were soft and warm, gentle. Noah pulled me toward him, his arms winding their way around my body. I slid across the bench easily, like I was practically weightless, until, suddenly, our bodies were pressed together. Even sitting, he was taller than me, so my head tilted back as his lips caressed mine. He placed a hand to support the back of my neck, as though aware of how much it would ache tilted at this angle. With his fingers in my hair and him all around me like that, my brain threatened sensory overload.

I wanted him, which I realized with abruptness—and not just in the stupid fantasies I allowed myself during workouts. I couldn't believe I hadn't seen it before, but I guess I'd been too wrapped up in the pursuit of Sean not to realize much of anything. Thinking about Sean didn't even distract me then, something I thought about much later, after I had time to process the fact that I had kissed Noah. But then, in that moment with Noah, I just closed my eyes and let myself melt away, thinking only one thought over and over.

Noah was *kissing* me.

Noah was kissing me.

Wait... Noah was kissing *me*.

And he was kissing me well, too.

When we broke apart, we each drew in a deep breath. As my lungs refilled with air, I couldn't help myself. The giggles broke through again—a silly schoolgirl with a crush on the popular boy in class. I felt foolish and I'm sure my blushing cheeks gave me away.

Noah smiled affectionately, the occasional chuckle escaping his lips, and shook his head at me.

"You're a raving lunatic," he said, kissing the tip of my nose.

The gesture was so intimate, so sweet, that I stopped giggling in surprise.

I tried not to gasp, but a tiny bit of air escaped my lips. I wanted to fall into him, squeeze him against me. I could even overlook that we were in a gym—of all places—and that I was not in any kind of condition to be so close to anyone at all, thanks to that run.

If he thought I smelled bad, he didn't give any indication. And to be honest, if he smelled bad—hey, he'd just run the same route of the Common that I had, granted it wasn't as much of an exertion for him—I didn't notice it either. Instead, I just took in that moment, that sweet exchange, and let it affect me. Overcome, I leaned in to him for more.

Just as our lips met for a second time, my phone buzzed in my pocket. I wanted to chuck it across the room and watch it smash into a million pieces.

"What was that?" Noah asked, pulling away. I have a special phone for the hearing impaired that buzzes pretty violently so you're sure to catch every single call, text, and alert. As it began to buzz a second time, I knew it was an incoming call.

"Forget it, it's just the phone." I leaned forward again, shoving one hand into my pocket to end the incessant buzzing, and very clearly indicated my intentions.

"But it could be Claire," Noah said in the midst of the siege I was laying on his lips. I pulled away, frowning at him. "What if she needs you to go pick her up?"

"Why are you so worried about Claire?" I snapped. Okay, maybe my sister was a hot button with me when it came to men. *I can't imagine why...* Noah clearly couldn't understand it either and gave me a critical eyebrow in response. "Fine, fine. I'll answer it."

I spun away from him and got to my feet. A mistake, since my knees had been sufficiently weakened by a certain trainer I know. I flipped open that phone, trying not to stumble, and answered Claire's call. It wasn't a broken ankle, just really sprained, and she'd be out of commission for three weeks, the doctors said.

"So stay with me, okay?"

"What? Jen, I can't impose on you like that..." she tried, pointlessly, to argue.

"You live on the fifth floor of a building with an unreliable elevator. Have Tom get some of your stuff together and bring you to Mom's—uh, my—place. No arguing." I snapped the phone shut on her and her horrible timing and turned back to Noah. He was just lounging there on the bench, trying to stay occupied and not listen in on my call. Even so, he looked up just as my eyes found their way to him. When they connected across the space between us, the spark was already fading.

"Go take care of Claire," he said kindly, rising to his feet. As he walked to me, I could feel my temperature rising, the blood vessels swelling in my reddening cheeks. So of course, I had to make it awkward.

"Yeah... I should go, I guess," I said, stiffening as he embraced me. It was a halfhearted effort on his part anyway. The moment was gone. Evaporated. I straightened, pulling back from Noah's taut form. "I have to...uh... let her in. To...the... thing."

"Your apartment?" He raised an eyebrow at my lameness but didn't further the issue. Instead, he leaned down for one last quick and gentle kiss, much shorter and with much less passion attached to it. This kiss served as an effective punctuation mark on whatever incredible sentence we had been speaking to each other. Before Claire called, anyway.

"I'll see you tomorrow, same time?" he asked, shifting easily back to Trainer Noah as though he hadn't just made me see stars with the power of his mouth.

I nodded. "I guess it's just me and you, until Claire's back on her feet." I was still seeing those stars, so it was impressive that I could string so many words together.

"There are worse things," he smirked, handing me my gym bag. I slung it over my shoulder and started backing away toward the door. I gave him a two-fingered wave and pushed my way through the door. He waved back, his eyes never breaking away from mine, not until after I had closed the door behind myself.

Shaken, confused, and extremely turned on, I made myself drive straight home without making an emergency ice cream detour. Claire would smell the sprinkles on my breath from a mile away. She might also, I realized, smell the distinctive scent of lies the moment I walked in the door. So instead of thinking about food, I concentrated on how in the hell I was going to act normal around my sister. With her living in my apartment, my life could get very difficult if I let it. No way was I letting her in on what had just happened, not when she was still fuming about Sean.

I tried to wipe away all traces of the post-Noah glow, and stopped for an iced coffee instead of ice cream. If I couldn't take a cold shower when I got home, I could at least drink something to shake out all that crazy hot attraction from my system.

At least until I saw him in the gym the next day, that is.

Back at my apartment, Claire and I were both mended up and working on our individual healing processes. Granted, I was much better off than she was, seeing as some antiseptic and a bandage had sorted me out. Three weeks would be a long time to fly solo at the gym, but after the day's activities, I was feeling good about my ability to make it on my own. Not to mention, looking forward to all the "private" sessions.

"Are you sure you don't mind me staying here for a little while?" Claire asked me again, as I placed her dinner on the TV tray in front of her. She was stretched out on my couch, icing her ankle, and I had actually cooked something that was both nutritious and delicious. "If I'm going to be in the way…"

"In the way of what?" I tried not to laugh too hard. Did she think I had a secret nightlife I'd never mentioned before? "I offered to let you stay here, remember? Tomorrow, I'll go get some more of your stuff and move it over here. But tonight, just eat your dinner like a good girl, okay?"

She nodded, silently, and picked up her fork. "Is this tofu, Jen? It is! Will wonders never cease?"

So my sister had now become my roommate, during the very week that I'd lied about having a roommate who didn't exist... but had a Facebook profile. I don't know what was happening in my head to convince me it was a good idea at the time, but there I was. Living a lie.

"So aside from the obvious male detour, how is the rest of the project going, Jen? What have your findings been so far?" I knew she wasn't trying to mock me, but the way Claire talked about my research sometimes made me seem a little ridiculous. Like I was goofing around in the backyard with a bottle of Diet Coke and some Mentos.

"Pretty much what I expected," I shrugged, content to keep things as abbreviated as possible on the topic, just in case she started getting any ideas about certain individuals I might have run into on Boston Common that day. It was bad enough that I was judging myself; I didn't need Claire jumping on board as well. "Guys like the hot chick, normal girls like the normal-looking girl."

"I enjoy that you classify yourself as 'normal-looking.' "

"Am I weird-looking?"

"No, of course not. It was just a funny thing to say."

"Yeah... hilarious," I rolled my eyes at her. "Anyway, the only thing that amazes me about this experience so far is how incredibly shallow guys can be. You wouldn't believe how many of them just send me message after message because they think I have big boobs and an easy button on the middle of my forehead."

"I'm pretty sure if there was a big, red button in the middle of your forehead, you wouldn't be getting any dates."

"Yeah, but an easy button, Claire? That's gold to these guys."

She sighed deeply and settled into the cushions of my couch. For a few moments, we just sat together and ate in silence like we used to when we were kids. Back then, I would wait for her to talk first, always taking the lead from my older sister. Today, I decided to be brave and shift us to uncertain territory.

"How are things with Tom? Any better?" I'd seen the way they left and drawn my own conclusions, but I was eager to learn her feelings were on the matter. Besides, what happened during and after that trip to the hospital anyway?

"Well, it's hard to say. We were a little distracted by the potentially broken joint, you know."

"No reason to be snippy," I pointed a fork at her, then ate the tofu square off of it. This stuff was definitely an acquired taste, which I had just barely begun to acquire. If only I could fry it in butter or something... "I am merely curious about whether you two had a chance to talk or to, ahem, *talk* things out at all. I mean, he *carried* you to the car like you were a little girl. It was freaking adorable."

"And kind of sexy," she grinned, blushing.

"Noah said he usually just calls the ambulance when stuff like that happens. But you got first class escort service, Claire. That's got to mean something, doesn't it?"

"I guess..." Claire thought for a minute, chewing slowly. "Did Noah really say that?"

I nodded, staring at her. I watched her processing the information, each emotion passing slowly behind her eyes. She really did care about Tom—although Lord knows what she saw in him—but I could see it all over her face. Tom was more than just another guy, another plaything to Claire. She'd been beating men away with a stick since long before Olivia had been deleting online messages from them and yet, Tom had done something right to capture her jaded heart.

Whether or not Tom wanted to capture it remained to be seen. I had my thoughts on the subject, but it wasn't my place to share them with Claire. Not now; not given how little I knew about him, or how little I'd observed the two of them together as anything more than trainer and patron. And there hadn't been even a peep from him in Olivia's message box in weeks, so I prayed that was over and done with.

"I finally asked him to dinner... so I guess that's something." Claire said it to the open space in my living room, as though this were an afterthought to an ended conversation. I jumped at this tidbit right away.

"That's great! What did he say? Are you going out soon? Where?" Some people have told me that I have a tendency to be overly eager at times.

"He said he'd look at his schedule." Her face fell as she said the words, again to the empty space in the living room. Depending on the guy, and his lifestyle in general, this could be a good or a bad statement. Time would tell with Tom.

But I swore to myself then that if he did anything to hurt my sister—anything at all—I'd rip his stupid muscles apart, one by one. With my bare hands. Because that's what sisters are for.

CHAPTER FOURTEEN

It didn't take very long at all for Sean to take advantage of the open door I'd left him on Boston Common. By the following morning, there was a lengthy note sitting in Olivia's message inbox and I had absolutely no idea what to do with it. I printed it out and brought it to class with me, hoping to have a little time to read through the three pages during a boring lecture or two.

It was him pouring his heart out, basically, and I was completely and utterly at a loss.

Dear Olivia -

It started off innocently and normally enough, but things went quickly downhill.

I ran into your roommate on Boston Common yesterday and it reminded me how disappointed I was that you couldn't stay very long at the party this weekend. I was really hoping to take some time to get reacquainted.

Anyway, I've been enjoying having a pen pal of sorts on the internet and I've missed it in these past few days. I hope that you find this note when you're back safe and sound from your modeling shoot. Would it be too forward of me to ask for pictures from some of your shoots? I'd love to see some of your work for myself, I bet they're all gorgeous. They'd have to be if they're of you!

Of course, if you'd prefer to meet me somewhere in person, that would be even better. You can bring your roommate along with you, if you like. She seems nice enough, so I wouldn't mind having her around if that would make you more comfortable.

I just can't stop thinking about you lately, and I don't want to miss out on a chance to find a real connection with you. I understand you're busy, so I am willing to wait for you and work around whatever you have going on. I just want the chance to talk.

Yours,
 Sean

I slid the printout into my notebook and tapped my fingers thoughtlessly through the rest of Dr. Chase's lecture. I had no idea what she was talking about. As my eyes wandered around the classroom, Lyla caught my attention. We'd been working as study partners all semester, and getting to know one another a little bit better, but we weren't exactly friends. She mouthed something about getting a coffee together after class and I nodded. I guess it couldn't hurt to talk to someone other than Claire for a change.

So we met up in the school's coffee house, stretching out onto a pair of leather love seats positioned conveniently in front of the fireplace. I let myself unwind a little as I passed Sean's message to Lyla and let her read. I closed my eyes so I couldn't see her reactions, which were no doubt animated at the very least.

"What the hell are you supposed to do with this bullshit?" She all but shrieked when she finished reading. "This is super sappy, Jen. I don't even know what to make of it."

"I think he's got it pretty bad for a fictional character," I shrugged. "I don't even know how that happened. We've just been talking on Facebook, that's all."

"Yeah, but about what?" Lyla did little to hide the accusatory tone from her question.

"We're not having chat sex or anything, for crying out loud. We just talk about stuff… I let him talk about his family, work, his goals, that kind of stuff. He just tells me—er, Olivia—things. And I answer him."

"See, that's your problem," said Lyla, handing the page back to me. "Hot girls don't let guys just talk and talk like that."

"They don't?"

She sighed deeply, cupping her hand around her forehead. "No offense, but for someone mastering in sociology, you've got no clue how basic social interactions work."

Lyla had a point. I could analyze entire cultures across oceans, centuries, and foreign languages. But when it came to how the real world operated, I was at a total loss.

"Yes, this is becoming more and more evident with every passing day," I said dejectedly. "So how do I get myself out of this?"

"Well, if you're determined to try to convince this guy that you're a better catch than Olivia…" Her voice dropped off, leaving her opinions on the matter fairly evident. "And Claire won't help you turn Olivia into a super bitch diva with a cold, cold heart, then I guess you just have one option."

"Which is?" I leaned forward, nearly spilling my coffee down the front of my new shirt.

"Keep Olivia out of the way, friend him yourself, and fill the void that Olivia's absence leaves. And if worse comes to worse, you can play Olivia online as an evil demon whore," she finished matter-of-factly. Then her eyes darkened and she squinted at me. "But I think you should just forget about him altogether. What's so special about this particular guy anyway?"

I hesitated for a moment, not sure how to answer. Had my friendship with Lyla evolved to a place where we could share heartbreak stories and secret past shames? Again, since I was so clueless about real social interaction, I couldn't say for sure. I had to give her something, though, at the very least.

"When we were in school, I had the biggest crush on him. I used to take the same classes as him and sit way in the back, just waiting for that one magical day that he would turn around and notice me sitting there. I had this fantasy that he would get tired of the popular girls one day and find me waiting there. I'd been there all along—just a normal girl who would love him like no one else could. All I wanted was for him to notice me. I was obsessed."

"Well that's not creepy at all…"

"It's not when you're thirteen. And remember, we didn't have the internet yet, so my stalking stayed in the classroom. I knew almost nothing about him outside of the persona he had."

"And you still don't," she said pointedly. I stared at her while she took a sip of coffee, nonplussed by my frustration. "I'm just saying…"

"But he was Sean O'Dwyer and he was handsome and smart and popular and athletic. He had all of these things, but no one who really loved him for who he was inside. I knew who he was, better than anyone else."

"How?"

"I found his journal one day, underneath his desk in geometry class. He didn't see it fall out of his bag, but I did, and I grabbed it on my way by. At first, I tried chasing him down the hallway to give it back to him. I thought it was finally my chance to talk to him… but he didn't hear me. All day, I couldn't get his attention and he didn't even know the notebook was missing. So, I… I took it home."

"And you read it?" Lyla nearly shouted, mocking me. "Jennifer Smith! That's dishonest."

"Nobody's perfect," I offered with a shrug. "But after I read it, cover to cover, I couldn't help but fall in love with him. He was so sensitive and so honest in that journal. There were poems and drawings. And he talked a lot about being lonely and how people saw him for what he seemed, not what he was. I knew I was better than that, that I could see Sean for himself. To know that he wanted that from someone, it really moved me…"

"Oh my God, are you gonna cry?" Lyla sounded shocked, but offered me a travel pack of Kleenex from her handbag all the same. I waved them away, forcing a smile onto my face to fight off my sentimental tears.

"Anyway, I had to leave it in the front office in an envelope to get it back to him, because I just couldn't get his attention. I don't know if I was just too shy or he was just that ignorant, but we never spoke. Not for years," I said, lost in thought. "Not until…"

"Until?" Lyla was hanging on my every word now, sitting on the edge of her seat. But I couldn't go on, I couldn't finish the story. Not in a coffee house, not right now.

"Hey, I've really gotta get going," I lied, checking the time on my cell phone. "I'm supposed to meet Claire."

Lyla groaned loudly, collapsing back into the love seat's plush cushions. "Come on!"

"Another time, I promise," I said, zipping my messenger bag closed. "Thanks for the coffee. I'll see you next class, okay? We'll do this again sometime."

"Fine, fine," she growled, waving me away. "But whatever he did to you, I hope it's not so bad that chasing him makes you an idiot. If it is, I'm out, girl."

Yeah, I thought, you probably will be. Especially when I told her who all that poetry was written about…

That night, I took Lyla's advice and commenced a plan of playing double agent against Sean. On one end, I replied to his email as Olivia and told him I was really swamped, out of town for at least a week, and with limited internet access. Genius. He wouldn't be expecting her to answer him back any time soon.

On the other end, I logged in as myself and sent a friend request along with a message:

Hi Sean,

Nice to see you on the Common yesterday. In case you forgot again—haha—this is Jennifer, Olivia's roommate. We went to school together too, so I thought we could reconnect.

Jennifer

Short, sweet, and to the point. If he bit, great. If not, I'd learn how to live my life without pursuing Sean. Somehow.

It took another day to hear back from him, but I was filled with glee at the words of his response to my friend request note. Not only did he accept as my new friend, but he had some surprising things to say.

Hi Jennifer –

Of course I remember you! Sorry about the other day—running into you out of context really threw me off. I'd love to reconnect and maybe even meet up sometime. With Olivia out of town, I'm sure you're in need of some company—haha. Let me know if you want to get together.

Sean

I stared at the screen for a long, long time, unsure how to proceed. This was unexpected. And really easy, way too easy. Either Sean really wanted to be friends with me now or he remembered me from our school days finally. Did he remember that journal? And the note that I left for him?

Dear Sean,

I understand how you feel completely. You do have a friend who knows you for yourself.

Jennifer Smith

I'd had those words emblazoned into my head for years. I'd fretted over them for days before leaving the journal at the front desk and for days after. He never replied, never said anything. I always thought I'd embarrassed him when he realized I'd read his journal. For that, I was sorry. But the insight it had given me was incomparable and I wouldn't have traded it for anything.

I wanted to go see him. Even if I had to confess that I was a huge liar.

If he got to know the real me, would that change things for him? Would he forgive me meeting him under false pretenses if he knew I were a good person in my heart? I wasn't trying to be deceitful, just trying to perform an experiment. Things escalated too quickly, before I knew what was happening. Surely, any normal human being would be able to understand how something like this could happen. But in order to get the truth to him and have him not walk out, Sean needed to get to know Jennifer first. And maybe fall for her the way I had long ago fallen for him.

If Sean finally saw Olivia wasn't everything he thought she was, would it be enough? I could be there, ready to pick up the pieces of him and save the day. He'd learn that I was the one he'd been interested in all along, not some Photo Shopped picture that I was pretty sure was disproportionate.

Determined, I answered him back right away: Sounds great, Sean. When and where do you want to get together? - J

CHAPTER FIFTEEN

The more time passed without a response from Sean, the more nervous I became. He wanted to hang out with me, then didn't want to make plans? People are busy, I get it, but come on. It had only been two days, so I couldn't say that he was really blowing me off... but it still irked me.

I had to fight off my suspicions that Sean's message had all been part of his own scheme. I'd been down this road enough to understand what could be going on here. Sean wanted to get to Olivia and so he was willing to go through what he thought was the closest channel: me. This had been happening in my life since grade school, when Jay Matthews asked me what kind of music Claire liked so he could make her the perfect mix tape. I'd been only too kind to oblige then, just happy that someone with such good looks as Jay would even talk to me, but that singular incident set a precedent for the rest of my life. Or, Claire's life.

In fact, Tom was one of the few men who didn't want me to help him get into Claire's pants. That meant he was either really interested in her for her, not for the sex, or he was such an egotistical maniac that he didn't think he would need any help capturing and keeping her attention. It was probably the latter, but it was still too soon to say.

But Sean, on the other hand, might be going about this the devious way. He would pretend to friend me, make himself look like a good guy--you know, friend of the closest friend, and therefore, eligible for dating or sleeping with—and wait to catch Olivia's attention. I'd danced this dance before and let me tell you, it hurt a lot more when you thought they were your friends and then they turned out to be using you. That even happened with a girl once, back in high school, who was convinced she could turn Claire to "the other side" and used me as her dearest friend and closest confidant while she staged her "coming out." That one stung quite a bit.

This time, with Sean the one steering the ship, I didn't think I could handle it. I knew how this was going to turn out and I didn't like it one bit.

Wait a minute, I stopped myself. I'm the new and improved Jennifer Smith now and this one takes no prisoners. What if I could turn the tables on Sean instead? He might be after Olivia now, but with me playing both sides, I had a real shot at changing Sean's mind about this whole scenario. Then, I'd just say Olivia moved out of town, delete her profile, and live happily ever after.

Sean would never know what hit him.

If I had Sean figured out by now, I had absolutely no idea what to do with Noah. One day, he's kissing me in the gym when no one is around to see. The next day, he's back to "professional" mode like the whole thing never happened. I wanted to tell myself that it was because we couldn't get a moment alone together, but not even I can fool myself that badly. See, he was going through the motions as usual, but there was something weird going on.

While it was nice to see Noah's familiar face at the gym, it left me feeling uneasy. I took less comfort as he counted out my reps and eyed my form. He worked me through our usual circuit with a quiet fire burning behind his eyes. He looked intense, totally swept away and in the moment. For a change, it made me feel like the one with even footing, like he was quietly hoping I had the answer to some desperate question for him.

After our workout session ended, however, I quickly learned what his fierce intensity had been all about.

"How's your sister doing?" Noah asked, passing me a clean towel to wipe down the elliptical. "It's been a whole week and I haven't heard you say a word about her."

"Well, she's not here, is she? Why would I want to talk about Claire?"

"Whoa, sorry," he said, putting his hands up in surrender. "I was just wondering how she was…"

Dammit. I should've known he was thinking about Claire, and how to get closer to her. He offered a nervous smile. "So, um… Jen. Do you want to get dinner together some time?"

I cleared my throat. "Listen, Noah, if you're looking for information about my sister…"

"Your sister?" He looked genuinely puzzled. "What are you talking about?"

"You know… hot guy meets my sister, who doesn't give him the time of day. Then I come along, the innocent, frumpy-looking sister…"

"Jen, you're not frumpy-looking." Noah said, his tone hardening.

I waved him off. "The point is, I know what you're after and I can't help you. Claire isn't exactly single right now anyway, so I can't help you get any closer to her. Okay?"

"What do you mean, she's not exactly single anymore?" His eyebrows lowered. "What happened?"

"She and Tom are getting pretty serious, from the look of it," I tried to stay nonchalant and shrug him off. His face contorted into an expression I couldn't read, but I could guess it was disappointment. I couldn't believe I'd been letting him use me, just like everyone else. "Have a good night, Noah."

Crossing the gym, I grabbed my sweatshirt from the coat rack and slipped it over my head. I was sweaty and sticky, but I knew how cold it would be outside, so the sweatshirt was a must. It clung to my skin, flattening my damp hair against the back of my neck. I tossed a casual wave over my shoulder to Noah as I neared the door. So when I turned back and saw him blocking the only exit, it startled me a little bit. I dropped my gym bag.

"How did you do that? I didn't hear you…"

Noah held his hand out, palm up, and unfurled his fingers. He was holding my hearing aids, which I'd left behind me in the rush. I snatched them greedily from his hands and turned my back to him so I could put them back in.

"Why are you ashamed of them?"

I bit my lip and turned to face him. "I'm not, okay? They're just… it's personal. It's like someone touching your deodorant or something."

Noah smirked, shaking his head. "Well, I like them. They make you different."

"Don't I know it?" I said sarcastically. "Listen, I really have to get going…"

"Please come out with me. I just want to talk."

"About Claire? The one who doesn't need help hearing you sneak up on her?"

"To hell with Claire!" Noah said, grabbing my arm. His gentle grip closed around my elbow, forcing me to look into his eyes. I'd never seen him angry before and I found myself fascinated by how handsome he could still be, even in this state. "You might find this hard to believe, but I want to talk to you. I want to talk to Jennifer."

"I'm sorry, Noah, it's just not a good time for me to be…" I blinked, searching my brain for the end of that sentence. For me to be what? What was I trying to get out of here? "To be… seeing anyone."

"What does that even mean?"

We stared at each other for a long while, as my brain did cartwheels around and around. If he wasn't interested in Claire—genuinely and completely not interested in my sister—this was a first. No one ever chose me over Claire. And even know that I was taking better care of myself, you'd think the last person to show any interest would be the guy who sees me at my worst on a regular basis. Trainers are supposed to be eye candy and motivators, not dating material. Right?

"I'm just... I have a lot going on right now." My eyes started tearing up at the thought of just how much. I couldn't explain to Noah that I was waiting to work things out with someone else. The words hurt too much to even think.

"So tell me about it," he said, his eyes creasing with concern.

I bit back the tears and shook my head.

He squeezed my hand, his eyes searching mine. "I'm here to talk, whenever you need it, Jen. I know you think I'm just some trainer, screaming in your face, but I'd like to be your friend too. If you'll let me."

"Can I hug you?" I said, suddenly, catching myself by surprise. Something about his kindness had opened something up inside of me. I needed a human connection, someone to understand me. I needed human contact, too.

Noah raised one eyebrow, considering me. "On one condition. You have to let me hug you back."

Laughing, I wiped away one stray tear with the back of my hand. I stretched up onto my tiptoes to reach my arms around his neck and squeezed as tightly as I could. Noah, his arms around my waist, was squeezing too, although gently enough not to crush me.

I don't want to sound like a creep or anything, but I'd never hugged a guy so muscly before. Even when we'd touched before, sharing that amazing kiss, I hadn't had the wherewithal to observe what Noah really felt like. His whole body was firm, but not overly hard. His skin still felt supple on top of the hardened muscles. I was nice and warm, encircled by his arms, safe almost. He made me feel so tiny, even with extra weight still on my frame. I felt like I could curl up here in his arms and be protected from everyone and everything. It was tempting, but it wasn't the plan.

When I let go, he didn't. Rather, he tightened his grip on my waist. I leaned back to look up at him, eye to eye, and smiled.

"Thanks for the hug, Noah, I needed—"

But I never got to finish that sentence, because Noah leaned in and pressed his mouth to mine. It was the kind of spontaneous thing that shouldn't have surprised me, coming from him. My reaction, however, was the surprising part. As soon as his lips touched mine, I felt something inside of me just collapse, like my heart fell out of my chest or my stomach bottomed out. A thrill raced through my body, and I had to try very, very hard to maintain my composure. I forced myself not to give in to my impulses, because it wasn't going to be pretty if I caved.

And as soon as I had the thought, I realized how wrong this was. Claire and Tom had started out something like this, and that wasn't the kind of thing I was after. The fantasies were fun, but they needed to stay fantasies. I wanted him to keep kissing me so badly, but I knew I couldn't let this go any further, not if I wanted to be with Sean, with a clear conscience. I pushed off of Noah's wide shoulders, breaking us apart.

Noah looked stunned, dropping his arms to his sides. "Jen, I'm sorry. I didn't mean to get so carried away. I swear I was just going to hug you."

"No, it's my fault. I shouldn't have…" I shook off one last tear as I flung my bag onto my shoulder. With my hand on the door, I turned back to him. "I really can't get involved with anyone right now, Noah. I'm sorry."

And I left him standing there, alone in the gym, as I climbed into my car and drove off into the night. I cried the whole way home.

While I hadn't exactly fully disclosed to Noah all my reservations about dating him, I hadn't lied about Claire and Tom getting more serious. What had started off as the old "let me check my schedule" attitude from Tom had become unbridled devotion in the days since. In fact, I kept finding him in my apartment, which was only slightly annoying. It was nice that Claire was so happy and finally seemed to be with someone who treated her right, but

Tom was just not among my favorite people. For my sister, I tolerated his presence.

And I just hoped they'd spend most of their time in Claire's temporary room... and out of my way.

That night, after leaving Noah behind me and fighting through a teary blur to drive home, I was especially thankful that they'd taken up residence in Claire's room with a DVD. That was about two hours that I wouldn't have to look at them being all snuggly and cuddly and gross on my couch. It was also two hours that I could dedicate to chipping away at my giant research paper.

Halfway through writing the section on Virtual Acquaintances: Real or Forced?, I clicked open a web browser to round up some information from my fake profile. Immediately, I was distracted from my work by a growing mound of notifications staring at me. I had messages, new friend requests, and a mountain of new posts on my wall. It was dizzying to see it all, and I couldn't help but wonder if this is what popular looked like all the time.

Maybe it was a good thing I'd survived life in anonymity for so long. It gave me the time to get good grades in school, at the very least.

So I waded through the pile, as had become my new Olivia-role-playing routine every few days when I went online. Most of the wall posts could be ignored. Heck, I didn't know these people anyway. I clicked through the Friend Requests and accepted them all without really looking. It didn't much matter at this point who I was or wasn't friends with, not really. And then I navigated my way to my message box.

First up, a note from Sean, asking Olivia if it was okay to hang out with Jen (yes, me) while she was away at her photo shoot. So this is why I hadn't heard from him since sending my last message. He was looking for permission? I typed a quick note—careful to keep it cool and aloof—and basically told him I didn't really care. Hopefully, this would plant the seeds of doubt that Olivia wasn't actually interested in him after all.

Next up, an even more unpleasant message from a far more surprising individual. Tom was back in action, it seemed, or had been within the last couple of days. Yes, during the time that he'd been necking regularly with my sister on my couch. Right here in my living room. He was checking in to see if I'd gotten his last note, sent sometime before he'd "gone on vacation."

Vacation, huh? "Family matters" my ass!

At a total loss, I wanted to throw my hands up into the air and walk straight into Claire's room wielding the proof of Tom's betrayal on my laptop. Except that I didn't want to give Tom the chance to talk his way out of this and convince Claire it was a mistake or something.

But then, it came to me. The perfect plan. If I could somehow test to see how Tom would react, now that he was with Claire, wouldn't my sister want me to do what was best for her? She could know once and for all if Tom was faithful, worthy of her. I'd want her to do the same for me.

So I replied to Tom's last message, putting on my Olivia thinking cap to properly establish the right tone.

Tom -

Sorry to have missed that party, and not to have answered you during all this time. You look pretty hot yourself and I'd love to give that *huge* something a try sometime. Do you think you'd still like to share with me? Or is it all eaten up already?

Although I was particularly proud of my crudeness, I had to cringe. Just a little.

Anyway, I'm dancing downtown next week at the Rock Club on Lansdowne Street and I'd love to get a drink with you afterwards. Maybe head back to my place or yours... wherever you think your huge something will fit the best. Let me know if you'll be there.

I thought for a minute, chewing my fingernail. That was too business-like an ending. I had to go over the top here, make it so that no self-respecting man in a relationship would ever accept this invitation. That way, I could be totally, 100%, without a doubt sure that Tom was a piece of scum.

Maybe I'll even let you talk me out of that bra.

Better. Not perfect, but much better. I signed it, *Yours, Olivia the Sex Goddess* and hit send. There was no way would he respond. It was too much. Way too much. Even a dense guy like Tom would see right through i.t… with any luck.

CHAPTER SIXTEEN

Once he had his precious Olivia's permission, Sean invited me out for a casual, friendly dinner at Chili's. So it wasn't the most romantic of venues—that much was evident—and he was probably not going to make any advances to sweep me off my feet. Still, it was the opportunity to get that one-on-one time that I'd so badly wanted for all of these years. Tonight was the perfect chance to show him who I really was and divert his attention from Olivia once and for all.

As I bustled around the apartment in a panicked blur, Claire sat on the couch with her arms crossed and an amused half-smile on her face. She didn't say anything, but her glaring eye was enough judgment on its own. I knew what she thought of Sean; I didn't have to ask. So I stuck my tongue out at her, told her to mind her own business, and then asked her advice on what I should wear. Hey, no man is an island, and no woman is either, okay?

Plus, Claire has much better fashion sense than I do. Just as a general rule.

She selected a black pencil skirt and a cashmere sweater set hiding in the back of my closet. I'd never been brave enough to wear before. It was a light eggshell color that I was convinced I would stain, and the v-neckline was more daring than I would have ever risked before. But now, with Sean's affection on the line, risks had to be taken.

I got to Chili's first, thank goodness, and had a few moments to stare myself down in the bathroom mirror. I thought about slapping myself once or twice, just to help my focus, but I didn't want to leave any handprints on my face. That might be a bit too weird, on top of all the other weird I was about to unveil to him.

Waiting in the lobby for a table, I saw him enter before his eyes found me. I was so anxious, and so excited to see him, that I forgot for a split second that he wouldn't be greeting me as romantically as I dreamed. My mind went blank at the remembered fact and I just stared at him, standing two feet away from me. He didn't see me standing there, or at least hadn't recognized me... again.

I cleared my throat and tapped him on the shoulder. He whirled around and locked eyes with mine. He faltered for a moment, then regained composure and offered a weaker version.

"Oh, hi, Jan," he said, looking around me. "How are you?"

"It's Jen," I corrected, as nicely as you can correct someone who has just forgotten your first name. Someone you have had a lifetime crush on and would like to convince to be crushing on you too.

"Sorry," he shrugged. "I really am terrible with names."

Except for the names of hot women who friend you on the internet.

"So how's Olivia been? Still out of town?" Sean asked, without skipping a beat.

My smile fell from my face and he saw it. "No, not yet. She hasn't sent you any messages or anything?"

Well done, Jen. Plant that seed of doubt.

"No, not really," he said, blinking.

For a moment, we just stood looking at each other. I'd spun yet another lie for Sean's benefit, and the guilt was starting to infiltrate my subconscious. Now was the time to tell him. Now, when he was quiet and looking at me, when we were standing here in person just inches from touching. But I didn't even know what word to start with.

"Come on, let's get a table," he said suddenly, pulling me from the depths of my self-loathing and guilt.

Sitting at a little two-seater table with Sean in the back of a Chili's was the way I'd planned it in my imagination. Crowded together at a tiny table where our knees touched, sharing our dinners with each other, smiling over a plate of nachos. Some of that stuff was actually happening in real life, including the bit with our knees touching under the table—my favorite part. The smiling happened on occasion and there were even nachos, but we hadn't quite reached the sharing food part yet.

"Olivia has only told me a little about you," he lied, loading up a nacho with sour cream. I happened to know first-hand that Olivia had never even mentioned a Jennifer or a roommate, but it was nice of him to make me feel included in his virtual relationship with my fake self. "What do you do for a living?"

"Well, I'm back in school right now," I said, pushing something Mexican around on my plate. After all this time away from sodium-laden foods, I was having a tough time eating the heavy faire at Chili's. Still, I took a bite every now and again, striving to at least make it look like I was enjoying my food. "I left my job as a Human Resources consultant to pursue a Master's in Sociology."

"That sounds... totally boring," he started to chuckle and earned a smile from me. "What are you going to do as a... Sociologist? Is that the right term?"

"There are lots of things," I shrugged. "I want to go back into consulting, but hopefully own my own freelancing agency. I'm specializing in interpersonal work relationships and modern communication. This is my last year so I'm—"

I froze, mid-word, realizing I was about to jump head first into a discussion about fake Facebook profiles and field research. Would he have figured it out that Olivia was my testing device? Probably not, not with me sitting here making up stories about her, but why risk it? I decided to dodge the conversation all together instead of letting too much information slip.

"Anyway," I shifted gears. "What do you do, Sean? I'm afraid Olivia hasn't told me much about you either." Might as well keep us on equal footing, right?

"Well, I'm a project manager for a landscaping company and I guess that's about it," he trailed off at the end. "There aren't any higher degrees required in my line of work or anything."

Sean actually seemed embarrassed about his job in front of me. I wasn't really sure what to make of that. Usually, I was the one being embarrassed about something, anything really. With the shoe on the other foot, how was I supposed to respond?

"At least you'll have fewer student loans to pay back!" I tried to smile at my poor joke, but not even I could muster a grin. Sean just shoved another nacho into his mouth and chewed. "Enough about work. What do you do for fun?"

"I like to go hang gliding when I can, and sometimes there's a rock gym I climb at on the weekends. Mostly outdoor stuff, if I can get the free time. Weird, I know, since I work outside too," he swallowed his nacho and considered another. "I just hate being cooped up inside all day."

His short list of hobbies was terrifying to someone like me, who often feared the bone-chilling heights of her parents' roof deck. I couldn't imagine jumping off of that with some metal poles and canvas "wings" strapped to my back. Hang gliding, huh? Does Sean have a death wish?

"What about you?" he asked, after a lengthy pause during which I stared down a clump of Mexican rice clinging to my fork.

"I don't have much time for anything else outside of school, but I recently took up running…"

"As I discovered a few days ago," he chuckled.

"Right," I laughed to hide my own embarrassment at that. "Well, I've been thinking about training for a 5K in the next couple of months. It sounded like a good way to get into running as a sport, not just as something I do to kill time." And burn calories, I thought but did not add out loud. My weight loss struggles were none of Sean's business and would hopefully be ended once and for all if he ever saw me naked.

I squeezed my eyes shut against the mental images entering my mind. All of this imagery just at the thought of the word naked... was I turning into a guy? I was at least, if not more, horny than most teenage males I knew as of late. Something's gotta give here soon, folks.

"Seems like you've got a good trainer already. What was his name, Nolan?"

"You really are terrible with names," I said, raising my eyebrows. "It's Noah and, yeah, he's the best."

He leaned forward, thrilling me beyond words. "So are you two... an item?"

I shook my head slowly, afraid to breathe too hard and have Sean move away from me. He really wanted to know if I was single, didn't he? A tiny part of me was upset at how quickly he could just forget how good a friend Olivia had been to him, but I didn't give that part much room to complain. Rather, I squashed it like a bug, choosing instead to blindly revel in the attention Sean was showing me. I might not need Claire after all, if I could kill off Olivia all by myself.

"He's just my trainer," I said after a moment, swallowing my nerves. I banished all thoughts of Noah's kisses, those piercing and intuitive eyes, and the way his butt looked when he...

"Good to know," Sean said, winking. When the waiter passed by the table, Sean asked for the check. He paid for my meal, like we were on a real date together here at Chili's, and touched my hand across the table. "What do you say we get out of here, Jen?"

Sean O'Dwyer held my hand (eek!) as we crossed the street and, although I knew my legs were working just fine, I felt like I was just floating over the pavement. I had no idea how I had gone from freaking out in the bathroom mirror about confessing my sins to this man to this, and so quickly too! Sean was turning out to be everything I'd always known him to be: funny, charming, kind-hearted, a kindred spirit. He joked lightly the entire walk back to my apartment, a path I wound him down without thinking. It was just so nice to get lost in his presence—his real-life presence, not just the imaginary version I'd been dreaming about for weeks—that the thrills clouded my judgment.

Before I realized where we'd traveled, we stood staring at each other in front of my parents' house. Oh no... it was time for a confession, before things went any further.

"Listen, Sean," I looked up into his eyes and felt myself weaken a little under their intense gaze. "I have to admit something. Um... this is my parents' house and I, um... live in the in-law apartment. I want to invite you in but I..."

Have a sister sitting on my couch. A sister that he cannot see again or everything is totally, totally blown!

"I don't care, Jen. It's fine," Sean said, leaning toward me. His eyes closed as his lips neared mine. I wanted nothing more than to shut my eyes too and just accept his kiss, let it erase what was left of my dizzied brain.

Instead, I put my finger to his lips. His eyes shot open. "Can you just hold that thought for one tiny second?"

I darted around to the side door of the house—my front door—and jiggled the key a few times, hoping to send Claire a signal. She was always acting psychic when it didn't matter, so could she just this once be legitimately telepathic when I needed it most? Please go and hide in your bedroom, Claire. Hear me jiggling the keys? Hear that? It means get the hell out of the living room!

Sean caught up to me before I could pop my head in to see if the coast was clear. "Everything okay?" he asked, brushing the hair off of my neck. I felt his hands brush against the skin beneath my ear and I panicked. Could he see my hearing aids in the dark? What would he think about me if he spotted them?

"Yeah, everything's fine!" My voice sounded shrill with anxiety, but I couldn't figure out how to shake my hair down over my ears again without looking like I didn't want him to touch me. I did so want him to touch me.

As I had the thought, Sean leaned into my neck and kissed it. I reeled with the tingling sensation, and pushed the door open before I gave myself any time to think about it. I lost my balance and fell forward, bringing Sean with me. We stumbled into my entryway, in full view of the living room, and the sister sitting on my couch.

"Jen?" Claire said cautiously. She was sprawled out on the couch, her ankle propped up on a bag of ice, and a Cosmo magazine spread across her lap. She was wearing a thick, pasty mask on her face, her hair pulled back in a headband, and she had a lollipop hanging out of her mouth.

"Where did you find my secret Tootsie Pops?" I said, my eyes narrowing on her.

"Olivia?" Sean had regained his footing and straightened up in the doorway, and was now staring directly at my sister. "Is that you?"

Claire looked stunned, shifting her eyes between Sean and I as though unsure what she should do. When I caught her eye, I nodded emphatically, pleading her with my eyes. Maybe her selective psychic powers would register this message, if not the last. Please, Claire, please!

"Hi," she said carefully, closing the magazine and stuffing it into the couch behind her. "Sean, right?"

Perfect! Keep it cool and aloof, Claire, and it's over and done with. Sean would get over her, get way into me instead, and we could finish our date properly. Claire and Olivia free. Alleluia!

Unfortunately, Sean was going to need more than cool and aloof to be shaken, once and for all. He darted across the living room and joined Claire on the couch, immediately laying a caring hand to her ankle.

"Does it hurt very badly? How did this happen?" he said, all the concern from the restaurant had been woven back into his tone. This was a completely different man than the one who had been kissing my neck ten seconds earlier. It had to be. No one was this duplicitous. "What are you doing back so early from Taiwan?"

"Oh, it's no big deal," Claire said, trying to shimmy away from him. "Just turned it wrong when I was working out."

"Do you work out with Neal too?"

"Noah," I corrected him again. Claire's head snapped in my direction with a questioning glare. I couldn't keep my seething anger from spilling over into my tone. Who could have?

"No, I don't," Claire said lightly. "It wasn't the trainer's fault anyway. I just stepped on it wrong."

"Well, is there anything I can do?"

"Not really," Claire shrugged, looking to me for back-up. I stood still, arms crossed in front of me. "I've got to get some rest, so why don't we call it a night? Jen?"

I swung the door open and held it for Sean. It took him a moment, but eventually he got the hint. He stood up and walked over to Claire, placed an awkward kiss on top of her head, and then walked back to the door, hanging his head low. He didn't look at me or say anything to me until he was most of the way outside, then he turned back and caught my eye.

"Night, Jan," he said softly. "See you around."

I slammed the door behind him and let out a loud sigh.

"What the hell was that all about?" Claire said, pointing to the empty seat on the couch. "Sit down and tell me what's going on. Why did you bring him here? And why am I still Olivia?"

CHAPTER SEVENTEEN

So I told Claire what happened. How close I'd gotten to distracting Sean from his fantasies about a girl who doesn't exist, only to be foiled by myself.

"Who brings a guy home to the very place he should not go? To the very person he can't see? I'm such an idiot, Claire," I slammed a hand down on the arm of the couch. "You'd think I'd never been on a date before."

"Well, it has been a while," Claire offered innocently.

I shot her a lethal glare. "Not the time."

"I'm sorry I didn't get the jiggling keys thing. I thought you were just struggling to get in. I was debating whether I hobble over to help you or not and then, there you were... both of you."

Closing my eyes, I punched the couch cushions. "Is it so much to ask for someone to like the actual me instead of the fake version? He couldn't even see your face and he just assumed you must be the beautiful, illustrious Olivia. She's not even supposed to be in the country!"

"Well, you told him Olivia was your roommate. Who else would be sitting on your couch like this?"

"My sister!"

"Look, Jen," she said, a warning note in her voice. "You were the one who created this imaginary world. This was supposed to be a project for your class, not a whole new problem to complicate your life. So just stop whining about it and fix the problem. It doesn't have to be this big of a deal."

"But I like him, Claire!"

"Do you?" She crossed her arms, studying me. It was hard to take her glare very seriously when her eyes were two white spheres amid the pasty, green face mask. "You like a guy who calls you by the wrong name, who interrupts his own make-out session with you to tend to your roommate's ankle, and who just limped out of here like a sad puppy dog when I told him to go home?"

I blinked at her wordlessly.

"A guy who broke your heart and…well, you know."

My shoulders slumped and I sank back against the couch. "Yes."

"Don't pout, Jen."

"Okay, okay. So he's not what I thought he was, all right? You don't have to rub it in. It's bad enough that everyone who meets you falls in love with you!"

"Oh, please. Don't turn this around on me! I didn't do this to you, Jen."

A knock came on the side door just then, the one connecting my apartment to my parents' home. "Everything okay in there, girls?" It was Mom, on a not-so-stealth mission to solve her daughters' every problem. She opened the door, which had no lock, and stuck her head in. "What's all the shouting?"

"Nothing, Mom. It's just Claire trying to ruin my life again," I sighed, playing up the brat angle for my mother's benefit.

"Again?" Claire shouted, trying to stand but failing and flopping back onto the couch. "When did I ruin your life before?"

"Do you really want me to list the occasions?" I spat. She didn't say anything, so I continued. "When you were born pretty. When every boy I ever liked preferred you to me. When you were born with perfect hearing!"

"Okay, Jennifer," my mother interjected, sternly. I half expected her to send us to bed with no supper or something, given her scolding tone. "That's enough of that. Apologize to your sister."

"What for?" I held my hands up, innocent.

"It's not Claire's fault that she doesn't wear hearing aids. Didn't we talk about that enough when you were younger? I won't let you make her feel guilty about what she has that you don't, just as I wouldn't allow her to make you feel bad about it." My mother pushed her glasses up on her nose and stared me down, waiting for that apology.

Instead, I turned on my heel and marched into my bedroom. "It's all about Claire! It always has been!" I didn't go as far as to slam the door, but I really wanted to. There was a certain satisfaction that came from a slammed door, one I'd grown to love as a bratty teenager. I couldn't let myself get too caught up in playing that role anymore, not as I was staring my late twenties in the face, I didn't wait to be totally pathetic.

But my point remained behind me, hovering in the room as my sister and mother exchanged frustrated glances. I knew what would happen next and if I were a betting woman, I would've put money on a knock coming on my door in three…two…one.

Knock. There it was.

"Jennifer?" My mother cooed sweetly through the door. "May I come in?"

I got up from the bed and opened the door. "I'm fine, Ma, I promise. Just being dramatic to make a point to my sister."

"I wish you girls could just get along," she said, chewing on her lip. I moved out of the way so she could come in and we sat next to each other on the end of my bed. "You're sisters, after all. And you need to be there for each other."

"We are," I said, trying not to get too defensive. I happened to think my relationship with Claire was one of the better sister bonds I'd ever witnessed in real life. "She just gets under my skin sometimes. I feel like she got all the good stuff and I got all the… crap."

"You know that's not true. Look at you, with plenty of smarts, a great sense of humor, lots of ambition. You're on your way to doing great things, Jen. You don't need some stupid boy chasing you around."

"You heard that, huh?" I stared down at my hands.

"These walls are thinner than you and your sister want to admit to yourselves," she said, suppressing a laugh. "The point is, there is more to life than a handsome guy who wants to kiss you. Your sister has had plenty of guys chasing her, but she's sitting in your living room, just as single as you are."

It was not the time to bring up Tom, so I let the comment go without a response.

"The difference is, all of those guys were quite distracting for your sister," my mother said, tucking my hair behind my ear. She said she liked looking at my hearing aids because they were a miracle that had helped her baby talk to her. "And Claire had her heart broken a few times by the ones who arrived in disguise as 'nice guys.' Take advantage of the time you have to yourself, Jennifer, and don't waste it wishing for things you don't have."

I sighed heavily, and my mother pulled me against her shoulder.

"You have too many things going for you to get bogged down by the stuff that isn't within your control," she squeezed me tightly. "The right one will come along, when you're not looking for him. Okay, honey?"

As my mother let herself out of my room, and then my apartment, I let her comforting words wash around me. Was there really someone out there who would like the Jen that I was, just as she was? Or was he just waiting for me to shave off the rest of these pounds?

Can't I just hurry up and get finished with this already?

"So that's what I interrupted that day?" my mom says now, grimacing at me. "I had no idea you were fighting about Sean again."

"Well, your advice was still sound, even without context," I shrug, smiling weakly. "It meant a lot to me what you said that day. I think it helped me decide what to do."

"That's something, I guess."

Mom shifts on the couch, pulling one leg up underneath the other. I can see she's getting tired, especially considering the lateness of the hour, but I'm so close to finishing… she'd never let me stop talking now. As she stifles a yawn, I consider where to start back up again.

"Let's recap," she says, propping up on one elbow and widening her eyes. She's fighting to stay awake and I love her for it. "Sean wants Olivia, who he thinks is Claire. Claire thinks she has Tom, but he's too busy stalking Olivia. You still want Sean, even after all these years. But this Noah guy is just sitting around, oblivious to all of this, wanting to take you out to dinner?"

I sigh. "Why does oversimplifying everything make me sound like an idiot?"

"Well, sometimes you just need to look at the bare bones of things to understand what's really happening…" she says, trailing off. I can't help thinking that I should've just gone to her for advice in the first place, months ago when this all started.

"As I was saying," I groan, attempting to get us back on track. I sit cross-legged on the couch and lean forward to stretch my aching back. "Tom finally replied that he would meet up with Olivia, so all I had to do was convince Claire to go out to the club with me and catch him in the act."

I pause, studying my mother's face for a reaction but she gives nothing away.

"And she did, saying it would be good for her to get out and about, stretch the ankle again. But in the meantime, while I was waiting for the big night to arrive, things were getting tricky in other areas as well…"

Sitting in Dr. Chase's office a few days later, I felt like an errant child getting slapped on the hand. So I'd gotten a bad grade on a quiz. So what? It was just a quiz and this wasn't high school. I didn't really have to prove that I understood a bunch of definitions about sociology to this woman, did I?

I knew damn well that I did, assuming I still wanted to earn my Master's degree with honors, as was the plan; I just preferred to play 'obstinate child' in these scenarios. And Dr. Chase was doing a good job at playing 'disappointed school principle,' so I worked with what she was giving me.

"I've got to be frank with you, Jen," Dr. Chase said, folding her hands on her desk. "I know there's something pulling your focus away from my class, and your studies in general, and I want it to stop. As your advisor, I can't just sit here and let you goof off for the rest of the year."

"I'm not goofing off," I said, a bit scalded by her tone. "I just got one bad quiz grade. One." I held up my index finger to reinforce my point.

"For some other students, that wouldn't be as big of a sign to me. But coming from you, it's too out of character to let it slide. What's going on? Is this project overloading you?"

I looked at her blankly, racking my brain for a constructive class-related response to that question. Blinking, I just said, "Define overloading."

She sighed, closing her eyes. "Is it the research aspect? Something about the field report? How can I help you to manage so that I don't have to watch you flounder for the rest of your degree process?"

"It's nice of you to offer, Dr. C," I wanted to sound polite, but tell her to leave me alone all at once. Claire was born with all the tact, so I worried about my ability to walk this fine line. "But I think it's under control. It's just become more involved than I expected, but it's nothing I can't handle."

"Well, I certainly hope you're right," Dr. Chase pushed her chair back and stood up. "But if it gets to be too much…"

"I know, I know," I shook her hand. "I'll be the first one knocking on your door."

She let me go without any further explanation and I was relieved to get away with minimal damage. No more surfing during class and blowing off study time to play Olivia online. No more wasting my time on idiot men and other fruitless distractions. Gym, school, gym, school. That is your life, Jennifer Smith, and you'd better learn to enjoy it.

Speaking of the gym, that afternoon found me back at Tom's Workout World and less than enthusiastic about it. Tom didn't seem motivated to train me without Claire present and Noah was off that day, so I wound up working out with some skinny, bubbly chick that I could probably have crushed like a whoopee cushion. I imagined she'd make at least a similar sound, too, were I to actually sit on her.

It was a good workout, that left me sweating like a pig at a roast, but it just wasn't the same. I knew I hadn't pushed as hard as I could have, that I had more energy deep down in there to burn. I'd found a way to access it with Noah calling the shots and, I had to wonder, would I learn how to do that on my own, without him someday? If not, I was just going to have to follow Noah around from gym to gym for the rest of his career just to keep the extra weight from my frame.

There are worse things that could happen, I realized.

It also wasn't as fun to work out without Claire by my side. Even though I'd have to watch her effortlessly kick the crap out of my numbers and all my efforts, I preferred to have her with me rather than the alternative. As weird as it all sounded, I just wanted things to go back to normal…

CHAPTER EIGHTEEN

Life had other plans, however, and there were plenty of other things that would need changing before I could even think about "normal" again. At the top of my to-do list? Busting Tom on his not-date with a fake Facebook persona that Saturday.

The Rock Club was not my scene, but with Claire in tow, I could at least be sure to get through the door. She didn't seem to mind coming along when I told her there was a guy I wanted to meet... once I promised her it was not Sean O'Dwyer. Rather, she was only too happy to help me get ready to meet him. I acquiesced and let her dress me, do my hair and makeup, and instruct me on how to properly flirt with a man.

"Just toss your hair lightly, like this." She demonstrated.

I tried it.

"You're gonna break your neck if you do it like that. Like this, Jen."

And we went back and forth like that for the entire T ride to Fenway Station. During the walk from the station to Lansdowne Street, Claire's tutorial shifted focus to "how to properly walk in heels."

"I really hate when these slutty girls wear these gigantic heels and can't walk in them."

I scowled at her.

"You're not slutty, Jen. Come on." She batted my arm lightly, then tucked her clutch up under her arm. "Walk like me."

She sauntered up ahead of me, her heel making contact with the gravel on a half-second before her toe, so her feet didn't clomp around awkwardly. Her arms swished back and forth against her hip-hugging pants and sequin top. Even her hips were involved in this delicate dance across the parking lot.

Just watching her made me feel clumsy and heavy.

"Now you try," she said, over her shoulder. She stopped walking and waited for me to catch up. I concentrated really hard on how to guide each heel down in front of the last, lightly sashaying back and forth as I did so. My arms didn't glide as easily and my ankles weren't exactly cooperating with the stilettos heels Claire had put onto my feet. It took about five steps before I almost twisted my ankle and fell over.

"Oh, Jen," she shook her head, visibly restraining her laughter. "You'll get it. Come on."

She linked her arm through mine and led me toward the club, as though she thought the power of her body's guidance would make me walk less like a bull. I'm not really sure that was the case, but I made it to the front door without any injuries. That's something, at least.

The bouncer took one look at Claire and stepped out of the way to let us in. He didn't even hesitate when he saw me, which I took as a testament to how hard I'd been working at the gym. In any case, we got in for free too, no cover charge at all. Going out with my super-hot sister had its advantages, I guess.

Inside, I immediately regretted my decision to set up Tom in a place like this. It was crowded and loud, with very poor visibility. If Tom was here, there was a good chance I'd never even know it. Now what? I scanned the room desperately, from the crowded neon-lit bar counter to the smoke machine spewing onto the dance floor across the room. Lights, music, smoke... and alcohol. Perfect plan, Jen. Perfect plan.

"Let's get a drink while we look for this guy," Claire said, dragging me behind her. I tried to stop her, arguing that the bar was way too crowded and we should wait for it to clear out.

"Have you ever been to a club before? The bar never clears out, Jen."

But for Claire, that didn't seem to be a problem. She scooted her way in between two big guys, who were only too happy to get out of her way. One of them even offered to pay for her, just like that. If I wasn't going to get a free drink out of the deal too, I might've been annoyed at how easy things always seemed to be for Claire. Just because she was pretty, life just handed her things. Not fair. But I pushed the thought away, accepted my Dirty Shirley (that's a spiked Shirley Temple, for those of you who prefer the hard stuff) and followed Claire back out to the dance floor. We found one of those tall tables without chairs available and Claire fought off a couple of would-be suitors, then turned to me.

"So where are we supposed to meet this guy?"

"I'm not sure..." I scanned the room again, finding only a tangle of sweaty bodies on the dance floor and a crowd of half-drunken onlookers. Did people really come to these places to have fun? "He just said to meet him here. What if he couldn't get in?"

I thought about the bouncer stopping Tom at the door. Would he pull a jerk move and keep him out, based on his looks? Big, strapping guy who could be the bouncer himself? I craned my neck toward the door instinctively, but couldn't make out any faces. A few people passed through the door toward the bar and then I caught the confused look of a tall man with black hair that looked an awful lot like Tom.

Show time.

I swallowed a gulp of my Shirley, straightened my spine, and looked my sister dead in the eye. "Claire, I'm going to do something right now that you might hate me for." Her eyebrow lifted. "But please understand that I only did this because I love you and want what's best for you. Okay?"

She nodded, skeptical, but followed me toward the door. Pushing through bodies as we went, I almost lost track of him and went right by. Correcting my course and moving fast, I almost collided with him. I reached out and grabbed his arm to keep from falling over.

"Jen?" he asked. "Claire! What are you doing here?"

"What are you doing here?" Claire asked, her voice growing edgy. "I thought you said you had a family thing to go to."

"It...uh...got canceled." Was it just me, or was he panicking? "So, I'm glad we ran into each other."

I crossed my arms, staring him down. "Tell her why you're really here, Tom."

He looked at me, blinking, as though he'd forgotten I was standing there.

Claire nudged me. "Stay out of this, Jen."

"I'm sorry, but I can't. Tom is here to meet someone. Aren't you, Tom?"

His mouth gaped; he was at a total loss. It was like he couldn't tell if he was busted yet or not.

"What are you talking about?" Claire scoffed. Then, as realization dawned, she grabbed my arm. "You were here to meet Tom."

"Sort of. Right, Tom?" I turned back to him, his mouth still hanging wide open. "Didn't you come here to meet Olivia?"

"What is going on?" Claire's voice had turned deadly. "What did you do, Jen?"

I opened my clutch, extracted the printout of our Facebook messages, and handed them to Claire. Her eyes scanned the words in wide-open shock. As she read, her fingers tightened on the pages, her knuckles turned white. When she was finished, I expected her to rail at Tom, drag him outside and break up with him on the spot.

Instead, her steely glare turned on me.

"How could you do this? Why would you do this?" Her voice was low, her words deliberate and slow. She crumpled the pages in her hands, her eyes fiery, and threw them at me. "You're my SISTER, Jen!"

And then she walked out of the club, leaving Tom and I staring at each other. His expression went blank for a moment then he opened his mouth to speak, caught my eye, and snapped it shut again.

"This is your fault, you scum bag," I said to him, keeping my eyes on my stiletto heels. "I can't believe you would show up."

"So..." He started to speak and I looked up at him. It was too loud in here for me to get every word clearly unless I could see the speaker's lips moving. "You're Olivia?"

Heaving a sigh, I pushed past him and ran out of the club, hoping to catch my sister. I'd achieved my objective, clearly, and shown Claire what a piece of crap her boyfriend was. But instead of her thanking me or even dumping him over it, she'd just left me here. Wouldn't she want to know what kind of man he was? Wouldn't she appreciate the efforts?

Why would she just walk away?

I didn't expect to get back to my apartment and find all of Claire's things missing. She'd stripped her bed, pulled her food from the fridge, and even taken down the wall calendar she'd bought me for my work desk. Claire had left the apartment exactly the way she'd found it: solely occupied. I assumed she'd gone back to her apartment, something she could've done days ago with her ankle now heeled. Why she hadn't gone back before, I didn't understand. Not that I minded. It was nice to have Claire living with me for these weeks. Already, I missed her.

In the next few days, I didn't hear a word from her. My mother had talked to her, so I took some small comfort in the second-hand report from her. Claire was back at her place, her ankle was fine, and she was busy with work. Too busy to make it home for Easter. Ouch.

I'd been to the gym a couple of times too, but Claire wasn't there. According to Noah, she had called to cancel her membership and tried to cancel mine as well. I didn't realize she'd been paying for me to have a membership all this time; I'd honestly thought Tom was giving us free sessions as a personal favor. She couldn't cancel my membership completely, but she did cancel the automatic billing to her credit card. So when I went for my first workout after that horrible night, I had to pay first. I'd have been happy to pay all along; that wasn't the problem. Rather, I knew how deep a wound Claire had sustained if she was doing petty things like this.

Tom and Claire were also over and, thus, Tom was refusing to work out with me at all. Not that I asked him too. I just happened to look over Noah's shoulder into the appointment book and notice that my name had a note next to it, written in permanent marker: "Do Not Schedule with Tom."

I guess I couldn't blame him for that. At least he was still letting me step foot inside his gym.

"What happened?" Noah asked one day, braving the inevitable storm of tears he must've sensed was coming. As soon as the words were out of his mouth, I was bawling. He pulled me to him--the first affection I'd gotten from him in weeks--and I just cried it out. When I caught my breath again, I looked at him.

"I can't talk about it yet, okay? I have to fix it first."

He nodded, because Noah always seems to understand me. I'm not sure how, he just does it. He didn't ask me again after that and I just pushed it from my mind, focused on writing my paper and finishing my last semester of school, and tried to keep to routine as best I could. What else was there to do, anyway? This would all pass eventually and Claire and I would put it behind us.

I just needed to give her some time.

CHAPTER NINETEEN

"That may not have been the best idea you've ever had…" said Lyla the next morning. We sat together in a local bagel shop, having breakfast over a round of intense studying. And by intense studying, I mean we were hacking through my life with a metaphoric chainsaw. My life, Lyla said, should have been her research project.

I reminded her often, though, that my life sort of had become my research project.

"What was I supposed to do?" I said helplessly, as I tried to control how much cream cheese I smeared onto my onion bagel. This was so not diet-approved, but I felt like I'd earned it. Hey, wasn't it better than skipping right to the breakfast pastries?

"For starters, you could've sat down and talked to her." Lyla took the knife from my hand when I'd finished and began slathering her own generous portion of cream cheese onto her bagel. "I hear that works better than embarrassing people in public."

"I was trying to embarrass Tom, not Claire." The words were muffled around my mouthful of forbidden breakfast carbs. Cream cheese has protein in it, right?

"I'm sure you did that, too. But making them face off like that…" she paused, chewing a few times before continuing. "It's just not cool, my friend. Not cool."

"Is that why she's mad, you think?"

"That's probably part of it. I'd be willing to be she's also a little pissed at you for orchestrating the whole thing."

"Well that's just not fair. He started it, Lyla." I wanted to shove this entire bagel down my throat, but realized that was probably inadvisable. Instead, I took a long chug from my coffee cup. Some of it dribbled down my chin and onto my open notebook. "I just wanted her to see for herself."

"I know, hon. And Claire will figure that out too… someday."

"Gee, thanks for the pep talk," I said dejectedly.

"Hey, you screwed up. We all do it at one point or another. Now, you just have to wait it out and give her a chance to let it go."

"Do you also write greeting cards? I think you're an untapped resource," I frowned at her.

"Don't shoot the messenger, my friend. I don't make the rules," Lyla raised her hands in surrender, and I let her off the hook for now. We turned our breakfast conversation back to matters of our education and left the life advice for another time. Mostly, I just didn't want to admit that she was right.

I knew Claire needed some time… And I especially knew that hounding her would only make things worse. In my mind, we'd be upset about the incident for a few days, maybe a week or two, and then we'd be able to hug and make-up. One day, years from now, this would be a great story we'd tell our kids and just laugh about together.

"Did I ever tell you about the time your Auntie Jen pretended to be someone else so she could catch my boyfriend cheating? No? Oh, listen to this…" Claire would say. I'd be right there, laughing along with her, interjecting the occasion bit of dialogue or impersonating Tom's deer-in-headlights expression.

One day.

Of course, I never in a million years expected Claire to retaliate. In my mind, I did for Claire what I would have wanted her to do for me. I'd exposed Tom for what he really was and spared her heartache later down the road. She would have stayed with Tom until she caught him cheating on her, maybe months or even years later. Was that really what she would have preferred? I knew I was in the right and she would see things my way. Eventually.

Instead, Claire hacked into Olivia's profile and had turned the monster against its creator.

I guess that's what I get for using the same password for everything.

The day I found out, I tried to log in and kept getting kicked out. I tried to reset the password and have an email sent to my own account, but that didn't work either. Claire had changed the email address to hers, so I couldn't do a thing about it. So I logged in as myself and tried to view her profile that way. First of all, I wasn't even friends with Olivia any more. She hadn't blocked me, but she had unfriended me... from myself.

The craziness of that sentence threw me for a loop, but I pressed on.

Olivia had uploaded some new photos as well--all of Claire. She'd updated her status pretty regularly and started writing some very smutty comments on a few guys' walls. Claire had assumed the identity I'd created and blown her up in my face. Scrolling through the rubble that was now Olivia's Facebook wall, my jaw fell open wider and wider with every line. And then I stopped scrolling when I reached one particular conversation, between Olivia/Claire and Sean.

SEAN: See you Friday, right? So glad you can come out finally!
OLIVIA: I'll be there. What should I wear for you?
SEAN: Something red and sexy. Hahaha Whatever you want!
OLIVIA: If I wear anything at all....

I wanted to vomit all over my keyboard. First, about the crassness I'd just read for myself. Second, because Claire was going after something she thought I wanted. Me, her own sister!

Well, if Claire and Sean wanted to be together, let them have each other. They were both stuck up, too pretty, and too freaking perfect to date anyone else anyway. Right? They deserved each other. What the hell did I care?

More importantly, why did I care?

So that's where I'm at, today. I've got one man convinced he's going to travel to photo shoots with me, another trying to kiss me in the gym, and a third trying to cheat on my sister… with me. And only one of them actually wants the real Jennifer.

My sister hates me, because she thinks I'm the one ruining her life for a change, and I can't find a way to show her that what happened was actually a good thing. If not me, then who?

My grades are slipping. My project is imploding. And my professor thinks I'm trying to half-ass my way to a passing grade on this project. If she only knew what I was going through, maybe she'd have a little bit more compassion for my situation.

Meanwhile, all those efforts to lose weight are being quickly derailed. I bought Twinkies at the grocery store yesterday and, I'm not proud to say, there is only a half a box left in my cabinet. I thought about torching the rest of it, but then I thought my parents might not appreciate me accidentally burning down the house.

Also, plastic wrappers smell disgusting when you light them on fire.

And since I'm too embarrassed to face Noah at the gym, I haven't been able to work out in several days. I can already feel my muscles atrophying as we speak.

How did all of this go so terribly wrong?

And how can I make it all right again?

When I come to the end of my harrowing tale of internet fraud and sisterly betrayal, my mother doesn't say anything for a long time. She sips her tea thoughtfully, like it's a fancy wine to be sniffed and considered. Staring at a blank wall, she just takes little sips and doesn't respond. For a moment, I think she hasn't heard a single word I've said. Just as I'm about to poke her to get her attention, her eyes shift back to me.

"So things aren't going so well," she says finally.

"And that's less than helpful," I snap. Catching her eye, I relax my fisted hands, stretching out my tightened fingers. "Sorry, mom. I didn't mean that."

My mother folds me into her arms, hugging me to her. She runs a hand along my hair, the way only mothers can. "I'm glad you told me everything, honey. I needed to know what's going on if I'm going to be helpful."

I sit there for a quiet moment, just enjoying the comfort of having my mother understand and not pass judgment. We both know there are things to resolve here, but she's handling it like a pro.

"I think there are some things you need to take care of, Jen," she says, matter-of-factly. She points to my chest. "By exploring what's going on in your heart."

"Okay…" I draw it out, expecting more.

"Let's start with this project."

I groan, but she keeps talking.

"You took a picture of yourself and made it look like… Claire?" she asks. I don't like her tone, but I nod anyway. "And then, you tried to make a man who was in love with a fictional person fall for you instead, by using your sister to be the bad guy and turn him down."

"When you say it like that," I sniffle, looking away from her. "It sounds…"

"It doesn't sound very good, that's for sure."

"I'm not a psychoanalyst, and I certainly wouldn't try to analyze my own daughter if I was, but..." Mom's eyes scan the blank wall, looking for the right words. "Jennifer, I think you need to take a good, hard look at yourself and how you feel about who you are."

I blink at her for a quiet moment. "Are you saying I need to change?"

"No, not at all," she tries to smile, but it looks weak to me. "What I'm saying is that you might want to spend some time thinking about yourself, doing something for yourself. You're young and beautiful..."

I snort, but she ignores me.

"And you have so much to give to the world. What you're doing academically is great, and your father and I are so proud of you. But, in the long run..."

"I should be more like Claire?" My voice is shrill, my temper rising.

"Jennifer," Mom's voice turns harsh in response, a well-practiced tone thanks to my rebellious teenage years. "You know perfectly well that's not what I'm getting at. I have two daughters who are very different and whom I love for their individuality. Claire does what's right for Claire. You need to learn what's right for Jennifer, whether it's a project, a boyfriend, or a new career. You're the only one who can get the answers you're after, honey."

I sink back into the couch, my hands falling limply into my lap. "So you think I'm just a big, giant mess?"

"I think you're a smart girl who needs to learn to love herself for who she is. There's a lot to be said for independence and self-confidence, Jen. And right now, with the way things are in your life, you've ended up relying on a fake identity from the comfort of your parents' house to build a social life."

"That's not true," I straighten again, genuinely offended. "This was for a project! And you know why I live here, Mom. It's because it makes financial sense, not because I'm dependent on you and Dad. Come on, give me some credit."

"I'd like to see you go out once in a while, make some new friends."

"I have friends!"

"Then have them over once in a while," she folds her arms, considering me. "Do something that makes you happy."

After a moment of my not saying anything, she leans over and kisses my cheek. Mom clears the tea cups away, loads them into the dishwasher, and brings me a box of tissues to dry away the tears from my eyes. I didn't even known I was tearing up.

"Jennifer, it's time to find out who you really are. I think you should consider moving out of here, into an apartment with a friend or something. You can't hide in your books and behind an internet identity forever."

I sigh, looking away from her, but don't try to argue.

"Think about it, okay?"

After she leaves, I spend a lot of time picking the lint from the afghan on the back of my couch, the only activity I can do to keep myself from thinking. I don't want to admit to myself that there's any truth at all in what my mother has said, but certain words kept echoing in my mind.

CHAPTER TWENTY

In the morning, with a fresh perspective on my life thanks to my mother, I decide to get up early and do something for myself, just like she said. I hop in and out of the shower, pop in my hearing aids, and hit the road, determined to make today all about a clean slate.

I text Claire an apology, since I know she won't answer my calls, and tell her I want to talk things out. That's all I can do for now, I realize, and I'll just have to wait for her to be ready to move past this. If she really wants to be with Sean… I can't quite think about that yet. The wound is still too fresh.

Regardless, she's my sister and we'll have to find a way to work around that.

In class, I dominate a discussion about social communication via email versus cell phones. It's nice to finally have some experiences to recount, for a change. I even find a way to work in some information from my research project about the differences I've observed. My comments earn a few smiles and nods from Dr. Chase, who lets me leave after class just like everyone else. No more detention from the principal, I guess.

Lyla, too, seems to pick up on my renewed wave of positive energy. She falls into step with me after class as I head down to the library.

"Well hello, Little Miss Sunshine," she smiles, patting me on the shoulder. "Did you take Auntie Lyla's excellent advice?"

"You could say that," I shrug. "But really, I'm just tired of feeling bad about everything. You were right about me making a mistake, but I can't do anything now but apologize and give her some time."

"Thatta girl!"

"Hey, Lyla..." I say, struck by a sudden thought. "There's no chance you're looking for a roommate, is there?"

"Jennifer Smith, you have impeccable timing," she grins from ear to ear. "How do you feel about living with a self-proclaimed clean freak?"

"Pretty solid, actually."

"Excellent! You're hired. My roommate moves out at the end of this month. I'd much rather live with you than some stranger from Craigslist," Lyla says, steering me toward the coffee house. "Isn't there a saying about that? The weirdness you know is better than that you don't?"

"Another greeting card?"

"If only they were scoring well in the test markets..."

I laugh with her as we head into the coffee house to discuss roommate things and plan ahead for the future. I've never realized before what I'd been missing out on by keeping myself so isolated from everyone. Maybe it's just Lyla that puts me at ease, or maybe it could've been this way all along... who knows?

There's one more thing I need to do before I can say it's been the best day of reconciliation and positive new beginnings in history... and it involved a stop at Tom's Workout World. Luckily, Noah is at the gym just as I expected. Even more to my delight, he looks surprised—and pleased—to see me turn up.

"You're back!" he says, striding towards me from the front desk. "I was starting to think I'd have to find a new client to fill your time slot."

"Sorry about that..." I grimace. "I'll have to repent with extra mileage on that treadmill, I guess."

"That's just the beginning of your repentance," he counters, a mischievous gleam lighting his eye.

I take a deep breath and exhale a sigh. Things might be a bit awkward after what passed between us the last time I was here with him, but it was a relief to see that he didn't want to make a fuss about it anymore than I did.

Without my hearing aids in, I spent a decent amount of time letting Noah kick my lazy butt all around the gym. He even sent me to machines I'd never touched before, yelling just enough for me to hear him without screaming in my face. It felt good to be back in the zone, clicking with my trainer like this, ready to tackle anything he could through at me.

And holy cow, am I going to have trouble moving tomorrow!

When it's finally over, I collapse onto the mat with my bottle of water and just exist for a few minutes. I breathe deeply to lower my heart rate, just like Noah taught me weeks ago when we were training outdoors, and close my eyes. The post-workout adrenaline pulses through my body, awakening all my senses and leaving me with a feeling of accomplishment like no other. It's no wonder I've been feeling so down and out lately; all I needed was a good sweat to clear my head.

The mat crunches quietly as Noah sits beside me. He gently touches a hand to my arm and my eyes dart open. "What's really going on, Jen?"

"School… family stuff…" I say, forcing a half-smile. "You know, life."

"Come on," he says, standing up. "My last client canceled today, so I'm taking off early. You're coming with me, got it?"

Too tired to argue, and a little bit intrigued, I accept and follow Noah to his car without asking any questions. He throws my bag in the back and starts driving. Staring silently at my lap, thinking how badly I want to take a shower, I don't even pay attention to where we're going.

I guess it doesn't really matter to me.

"Are you hungry?" he says after a few moments. I've grown oddly comfortable in the silence, so the sound of his voice startles me out of my daze.

"Uhhh… no, not really. I can never really eat anything substantial after a workout."

"Want to get a coffee or something instead? I'm not really hungry either."

"Sure." I look out the window, watching the street lights blur against the snow-covered scenery. Noah stops in at a Dunkin Donuts drive-thru and buys two medium hot chocolates with whipped cream. Aww, sweet.

"Thanks, Noah," I offers him a genuine smile as he passes me one of the Styrofoam travel mugs. "Where did you want to go with our drinks?"

"I've been avoiding saying 'your place or mine' for this entire car ride, but to be honest, I can't think of anywhere else. I'm sure neither of us really wants to go anywhere in public after a day at the gym."

I laugh at his blunt honesty, and decide to extend the invite to my apartment. At the very least, I can sneak in a shower before we decide to go out somewhere or… I don't know. I don't know what I expect to happen, but I know I should be prepared for just about anything. Noah is full of thrilling surprises, so I've been learning.

Back in my apartment, which still feels eerie without Claire in it—weird how a temporary guest can shake things up like that, isn't it?—we sit down at my kitchen table with our hot chocolate and stare at each other. I try clearing my throat to get him to talk, pick at the plastic tab on the top of my hot chocolate, even tap the table with my fingertips.

"Noah…" I finally say, my impatience growing into something more lethal. "What's going on?"

Our eyes connect for a moment, across my rickety kitchen table for two, and then he looks away just as suddenly. When he does finally speak, it isn't in regards to anything I anticipate.

"What happened between you and Claire?"

"Me…and Claire?"

"Yeah, the two of you were so close. I would've never thought to see the day you weren't speaking. If it's none of my business, just say so. But as your friend…" His eyes seek mine as his voice trails off. I nod for him to continue. We can be friends and that's fine by me. "As your friend, I can't just sit by and watch you both implode. It's going to start affecting you, and not just in the gym."

"Is that what you're worried about?"

"It's not the only thing, or even the most important. It's just the one aspect of your life I can guarantee I'll be there to witness." He stands up, abandoning his empty cup on the counter, and starts pacing the tiny square of space in front of the sink. "So what happened? Was it Tom?"

"Kinda." I shrug, for lack of a better answer to that question.

"Did he… try anything with you?"

"Well, not exactly," I look away from him. His pacing makes me nervous and these questions aren't going somewhere I'm ready to bring Noah. "It's kind of complicated and I'm not sure—"

"Jesus, Jen, I have to work with the guy. No, for the guy. If he's messing around with the customers, I can't just stand by and let it happen. First Claire and then you, I just…" He trails off, looking to me for the answers.

"Look, it wasn't like that, okay? Tom's an asshole, but he's not messing around with the customers," I pause, not sure where to go. Noah's furrowed brow tells me he needs to hear more to be satisfied. But there isn't a good way to explain this, except to start from the beginning. "I'm a Sociology student, okay?"

Noah blinks. "What has that got to do with anything?"

"It features prominently, trust me," I say, sighing. "Do you want to hear the story or not?"

He nods and then listens. About halfway through the story, somewhere around the part where Sean thinks Claire is Olivia, he sits back down in the kitchen chair. Otherwise, he does a good job keeping his own personal feelings on the subject under wraps. I'm really sure what his response will be when I finally stop talking, but I know that I'm nervous it won't be favorable.

"So that's it," I say, talking to my hands. My hot chocolate has grown cold, my emotions thin. Until telling the story a second time, I didn't realize how much the experiences of the previous couple of months has affected me. Mostly, I'm exhausted, like I can curl up on my couch and sleep for several days. I also feel cold and distant, like I've been living in a cave. I never wanted to be so isolated, especially because of a stupid class project. As I study the skeptical look in Noah's eyes, I have to add, "I hope you don't hate me like everyone else."

"Hate you?" he bites back his laughter, at least, but the amusement in his face is clear. "Why would I hate you, Jen? You didn't do anything to me."

I swallow my defensive retort. "But... you think I do deserve to have everyone else mad at me?"

"No, not really," he shrugs. "People make mistakes. You got a little carried away, but you didn't really do any harm. Maybe she just didn't expect your project to affect her like that. But if it hadn't been you—er, Olivia—that Tom propositioned, it would've been some other girl. Someone Claire might never have known about."

Noah was pretty wise, and understood how these interpersonal relations worked, maybe better than me, the constant student. I'm so grateful, I don't know how to express it.

"There is one thing that does bother me, though," he says, narrowing his eyes. "This Sean guy... what's the real story there? He's the one from the Common, right?"

Apparently, Noah's got a better mind for names than Sean does, that much is clear. "Yeah, that's the same one... and to answer your question, there's nothing going on between us. He's with Claire now, or at least as far as I know."

As much as I want to keep Noah in the dark about my past with Sean, the probing questions he starts to ask are leading me down the road less traveled. Well, not traveled at all, actually. I've never told anyone about what happened all those years ago. As Noah asks why Sean mattered so much, what happened between us, and things like that, I can't keep him satisfied.

"You don't have to tell me anything, you know, Jen," he finally says, sighing in defeat. "But it really matters to me... personally."

I see it in his eyes before his words become clear. Noah likes me... no, more than that. Noah's interested in me and he wants to know where my heart is at too. Of course, he should be nervous after hearing a story like the one I just told. I'm surprised he's handling it so well, actually.

"He broke my heart," I blurt out, motivated by the feelings I see in Noah's eyes. "He was the first guy I ever liked. It was a long time ago."

"What happened?" The question takes all of his courage, I can see. He swallows hard, watching me for a reaction. Maybe even praying to himself that I'll answer him.

"I was a love-sick teenager and thought I had a special connection with him, but I was wrong…"

He nods, taking my hand in his. The sensation of his warmth, his skin touching mine, it inspires me to tell him everything.

"It was years before he even noticed I was alive. Then, one day, just before prom, he visited my locker. He brought me a rose and asked me out to dinner. I thought I'd died and gone to heaven, I was just so happy to be noticed… but not just noticed, either. He wanted to take me out on a date!" I cringe at the memory. Noah squeezes my hand and I continue. "I should've known something was wrong when he looked over at a group of the other jocks and winked. They were rolling with laughter… Stupid me, I thought he was asking me out despite them, not to have a good laugh with his buddies."

Noah shifts in his chair, his brow furrows. He's actually upset with Sean about this, and the thought comforts me. Noah would have protected me, would have fought to stop all the teasing. Where was Noah when I was a teenager?

"I went out to dinner with him and he was so sweet, holding my hand and smiling at me. He drove me home and played total gentleman, opening my door for me and walking me to the porch. I couldn't believe how lucky I was! And then, just as he leaned in to kiss me, the front door flew open. It was my sister and she was fuming."

"Claire?" Noah whispers.

"Only sister I have," I say, smiling weakly. "Anyway, she screamed at him. 'How could you do this to her?' and 'This isn't what I meant at all!' and 'You're disgusting, get out of my house.' The whole time, Sean's just gaping at her. He stands there until she finally runs out of steam and shrugs his shoulders. Then he said…"

I take a deep breath, not willing to relive this painful moment. Noah wipes a stray tear from my cheek with his thumb. "It's okay," he says quietly, kissing my forehead. "You don't have to…"

"No, I do," I choke out the words. "I need to tell someone. It's been long enough."

"Okay," he resigns. "What did he say to you?"

"He said, 'I only took this cow out for dinner because I thought it's what you wanted, Claire. You said if I could prove I was a nice guy, you'd go to prom with me…' It was so blunt, I didn't know what to do. After that, I locked myself in my room and just cried for the rest of the weekend. That's when I started hiding Hostess cupcakes in my sock drawer, too."

"Oh, Jen," he says breathlessly, gathering me against his chest. I let the last of my tears fall onto his shoulder. They absorb into the cotton of his t-shirt, temporary proof of my pain. "Oh, Jen."

"You want to kill him don't you?" I sputter the words out, a lame attempt at a joke.

He chuckles, deep in his chest. "Maybe later," he says. "But right now, I had another plan in mind."

At first. Noah's kiss is intense, but nothing I can't handle. At least, not until he gently moves my lips apart and slides his tongue against mine. It's enough to break the dam of my self-control, and there's nothing I could do to stop myself after that. In one fluid movement, I wind my arms back around his neck and hop up onto his waist. I don't give him any warning, but Noah doesn't need it. He catches my legs on either side of his hips, supporting my weight around his waist—like we've planned for this to happen or something.

Noah stumbles backwards as he adjusts his balance, and slams back against my kitchen counter. He sends several things flying in all directions, but neither of us is bothered by the clatter. We just keep kissing each other as though our lives depend upon this passionate connection, like we'd wither up and die if we broke apart. It feels nice to see so much of my own need reflected back at me, to be the one needed by another.

A sigh escapes my lips then and Noah's mouth grows hungrier for mine. He presses toward me so hard, we almost lose balance again and, this time, stumble into the kitchen table. My half-drunk hot chocolate flies from the table, exploding its contents all over the wall. Neither of us care very much about this at all. We notice it happen, then leave it to harden and dry on the yellow-tiled wall.

I know, however, that if we carry on this way, either one of us would wind up injured or my mother will let herself in to see what the racket is all about. Quite frankly, neither of those options appeals to me. So I break away from him, long enough to exclaim a quick, "Wait!"

"What? What's wrong?" Noah lets go of me immediately, guiding my feet back to the dirtied kitchen floor.

I giggle, like I'm frickin' twelve or something.

"Why are you laughing?" His face falls.

"Well, we've kinda destroyed my kitchen," I say, shrugging. I smile playfully so he can see I'm not exactly upset about it. "And I just thought it might be safer for all parties involved if we went somewhere with more space."

As the words sink in, Noah returns my playful smile. "Oh, I see," he says, leaning in to kiss me again. "Then let's continue this conversation elsewhere."

A moment later, I find myself hanging over Noah's shoulder like a rag doll. I laugh even as I wriggle to free my legs from his grasp. "Put me down!"

"I'll put you down," he says, fighting to keep a serious tone in his voice. "As soon as I find a good spot."

Noah marches around my little apartment with me slung over his shoulder and makes a big production of searching for more space. "Well this room is far too tiny," he declares, standing in my living room. "That TV doesn't stand a chance. How about in here?"

He pokes his head into my bathroom. "Oh no, this won't do at all. Far too many hair care products."

Next, he sticks his head into the extra bedroom, where Claire had been staying on the pull-out couch. Upside down, I peek around Noah's shoulder into the room. As he pushes the door open, I half expect to find Claire sitting there. But the room is dark, the bed folded away, and all of her things have been removed. It hurts all over again.

Noah, ever compassionate Noah, feels the change in my demeanor almost as soon as I do. His shoulders slacken and he puts me down, cupping his hands around my chin.

"What's wrong? Did I do something?"

I shake my head as one tear rolls from my eye. I hope the movement can shake it free and, foolishly, I thought he might not see it. I am, of course, busted.

"Here, now," he says, swiping a finger across my cheek to knock the tear away. "This does not seem like the right time to start crying. I might take it personally, you know."

Despite myself, I laugh at his bad joke. Leave it to him to lighten the mood all over again. I can let myself forget all about Claire for one night, I decide, staring into his blue eyes. I deserve a little time to treat myself. Hadn't my mother told me those exact words?

Why the hell not?

"You know," I say, suppressing a mischievous grin. "I'm feeling better already."

He can't hide his own matching grin, which thrills me beyond belief.

"Let's just stay out of that room," I advise.

"So where to?"

I wind my fingers between his and tug his arm. He's relaxed enough that I can jerk him towards me a little bit. We take the five or so steps down the tiny hallway. Standing in front of my bedroom door, staring up at Noah, I have no more reservations left in me at all.

He slips his arm behind me to turn the doorknob and open the door, and I reach up to kiss him again. Our lips connected, our bodies moving together, I pull him with me through the doorway.

Noah wants me. Not Olivia. Not Claire.
Just Jennifer.
So I let Noah show me just how badly he wants me.

CHAPTER TWENTY-ONE

From way up here on happy cloud #9, things were finally starting to look up. In fact, I got pretty confident that there would be only good things in my future, no more bad. How could it really have gotten worse, anyway?

But alas, things can always get worse. And, for the record, I've noticed that they tend to get worse just when you start to observe that they couldn't possibly do something like that. Never tempt fate or challenge God or whatever you want to call it. Just don't. Because what they say is true: when it rains it pours.

If only it was raining tonight, it would have been perfect. Like one of those frickin' movie scenes where the heroine's life all implodes right in front of her very eyes and there's not a damn thing she can do about it. The hero walks away, leaving her in the rain, holding the dog's leash or something. Wilted flowers, maybe. Anyway, there's no rain. And besides, I'm indoors so it would be totally irrelevant even if it were raining.

Focus, Jen, focus.

So a couple of weeks after my amazing night with Noah, I'm just minding my own business, typing away on my paper. I'm getting really close to the end, just a few pages left to go and then I can write a killer conclusion, edit the crap out of it, and probably pass it in a few days early. Rock on. So I'm typing, no one's around. Even my parents are out for the night, which never happens. Maybe I should have been suspicious, just based on that fact alone.

I answer the door and get the shock of my life when I see Sean standing there. Not drenched from the rain, of course, but standing there looking emotionally drenched. If there is such a thing.

"Jen," he says, pushing past me into the room. I don't recall inviting the man who fell for my imaginary personality and thus my sister into my home, but here he is. Sitting on my couch? Why is he sitting on my couch?

"What are you doing here, Sean? This isn't a good time for me, okay?" The last thing I want is to be alone with him in my apartment. I'm with Noah now, no more time for stupid high school games. But looking at him, the wound still smarts. And to be frankly honest, I just don't trust myself when faced with him, yet. He's so handsome and looks so sad, like a little Pound Puppy toy or something.

"I don't have anywhere else to go! She left me, Jen," he sighs, apparently near tears. "You have to help me get her back."

"You came here because of Claire?"

"Claire?"

Oops. Cover blown. Lucy has some 'splaining to do, that's for sure.

"Um... Olivia, I mean."

"Who the hell is Claire?"

"That's just what I call Olivia. It's a..." What was that word? "A nickname. It's a nickname."

"Whatever," he says, getting comfortable. He stretches one arm along the back of the couch and gestures for me to sit with him. "Come talk to me."

"I would really prefer it if you just left. Now," I cringe. "I can't help you with Olivia. We're not speaking anymore."

"Really?" He doesn't seem very disappointed, mostly just interested. "Why?"

"It's a long story, but we had a big fight over something stupid." I can't exactly tell him the truth, now can I? Sean's ego is already big enough for about three men, so why on earth would I ever give him more of a reason to think he was God's gift to women?

"Was it about me?" He asks, almost playfully. Beneath the flirty grin, I detect a hint of honesty. See? He really does have a huge ego, after all. And having him sit there, looking at me as though I were an all-you-can eat buffet table, I suddenly realize how stupid it was for me to try to get anywhere with a guy like this. How is he any different than Tom?

"Of course not," I answer too quickly. He responds with a knowing grin, patting the couch again for me to join him. "I'm good over here. Standing."

"Suit yourself." He stretches out, curling his arm up and tensing the muscles. Ass. Get off my furniture. I cross my arms and try to stare him down as evilly as I possibly can.

"Can you please leave?"

"Not until I get your advice," he says, dropping the macho act. "Olivia said she couldn't be with me anymore and I need you to help me figure out why."

I stare at him.

"So I can get her back."

I sigh. "Fine, Sean. Talk."

He tells me some elaborate story, whereby Olivia—or rather, Claire—went on a few dates with him, never put out, wouldn't even let him kiss her, and then suddenly, called it all off. Sean is surprisingly detailed in his account, despite the fact that I'm actually a woman and do not care about how "Olivia was showing off her tits" on the second date.

"So that was it," he throws his hands up. "She just said that she'd gotten what she wanted and it was all over. That was that. Done. I haven't heard from her in about two weeks."

"Two weeks?" I blink, mulling over all the information Sean has just dumped onto my couch cushions with the grace of an elephant dancing ballet. "This happened two weeks ago?"

"Yeah… Is that important?" He sits up. "Do you know why she stopped talking to me? Was it her period or something?"

I groan audibly before opening the door and holding it for him. "Come on, out with you. Playtime's over. Out!"

"What's going on here?"

I blinked a few times just to be sure Noah is really standing in my doorway.

"Um…hi," I muster. "Sean was just leaving."

Sean stands up from the couch then, careful to push his way right in between Noah and I. "Trainer Nolan, right? What are you doing here?"

"It's Noah," I say through gritted teeth, trying to push him out of the way.

"What's going on here, Jen?" Noah asks, stepping to the side so he can see me. "Is he bothering you?"

"No, it's fine," I say, hands on my hips again. "Right, Sean? You're leaving now."

"All right, all right!" He holds his hands up. "I'm gone. Just… tell Olivia I stopped by."

"I will do no such thing." I slam the door in his face.

"Everything okay?" Noah says, taking my hand to lead me to the couch. "What was he even doing here?"

"Trying to get to Claire…er, Olivia. I guess some things never change. But, as you know, I can't exactly help him on that front."

"I don't know why you would even if you were talking to Claire right now," he says. "Is this something you're well practiced at?"

"Guys have always come to me to get to Claire. That's why I thought you… That day you asked me to dinner and I…"

"I was never after Claire," he says, leaning in for a kiss. "I only had eyes for you."

"Aww, cute," I say, straightening up. "You know, he did say something odd though. About what happened between him and Olivia."

"Claire."

"Right. Sorry." And I tell him about their fake relationship, with no physical contact at all, and the abrupt end two weeks ago. "It's like she was up to something."

"I think you should call her and tell her that he came by here," he offers, stroking my hair.

"She's not going to talk to me, Noah."

"How can you be so sure? It sounds to me that she was doing for you what you did for her with Tom."

I push my left hearing aid in a little further and grimace at him. "Huh?"

"Think about it, Jen," he says, thoughtfully. "You set her up with Tom and she takes off. The next thing you know, she's retaliating… or you think she's retaliating… by hijacking Olivia's profile and taking Sean's attentions away from you. With him out of the way, think about how much you've been able to grow and start doing things for yourself."

"Like you?"

"Well, I suppose yes, you've been able to start doing me for yourself. But I wasn't going to be so crude as that, Jen. My goodness."

I laugh, giving him a kiss on the cheek. But I consider his words, because after all the years of knowing Claire, it seems like exactly the type of evil scheme she would concoct in that deranged head of hers. And the timing works too.

It was two weeks ago that Noah and I first spent the night together.

Now, it would be a little creepy if Claire knew the details of my sex life that intimately, but she isn't stupid. And she has ways of getting information. It might be that she knew Noah and I were spending time together outside of the gym and, that being enough to convince her that I'd moved on, she let Sean go. Out into the wild, she would've said. To torment other women of the world, and leave her sister alone.

I guess it was all just a matter of how you looked at it, but my gut told me that Claire was trying to clear a path for me to find myself, Noah, or maybe just a new social life outside of my computer habit. What a good sister she was, after all.

"I think I do need to call her," I say, sitting up straight.

He smiles at me, but it has a mischievous edge to it. Noah leans in to me, his lips lightly brushing my neck and collarbone. "Do you have to call her right this minute?"

I sigh deeply, leaning back into the cushions of the couch, and let his fingertips move underneath my t-shirt and across the skin of my stomach. I even fight the urge to suck it in. With Noah, there's no point in keeping up appearances. No point putting on airs. He already knows what I looked like at my heaviest, without makeup on, and sweating buckets through my shirts.

In some way, there was a certain freedom involved in dating your trainer. That's not really something you think about, but there it is. And for me, that freeing spirit is just the thing I needed to really unwind and just be plain old Jennifer around him. I could see myself easily becoming addicted to this feeling in the future.

Afterwards, we cuddle on the couch together with a thin afghan to protect us against the chill of the room. I look up at him, his arm wrapped around me, and grin like an idiot. I'm in love with Noah and he's in love with me. I know it already.

"Jen..." he says suddenly, his tone turning serious. "You and Sean, you never..."

"Nothing ever happened there, okay? Well..." I pause, and it hits him like a ton of bricks.

"What?" He leans away from me.

"Before you and I... you know," I struggle with it, desperate for the words. "There was one night that Sean tried to bring me home. But it was only to get to Claire, which I realize doesn't make sense. But... I didn't do it, okay?"

His expression hardens as he considers me. "Nothing?"

"We... made out a little bit," I look away. "And I might have invited him in."

"Jen," his voice turns cold.

"But then Claire was sitting here, and he thought she was Olivia and then he didn't want me anymore. And so nothing happened..."

"If Claire hadn't been here and Sean had still wanted you, you would have..."

"Yes!" I say, standing up and taking the afghan with me. I wrap it like a shawl around my shoulders. "I would have, because I had no self-esteem and I thought he was the kind of guy that I wanted!"

"Okay, fine." His eyes remain steely. "I think I'm going to get going, okay?"

Wordlessly, he picks up his clothes from around the room and gets dressed slowly. I watch him, helpless and unable to speak. I pull the blanket around me tighter and try to pretend I don't care.

"That was so long ago, Noah. I don't know why you're so upset about this."

"Because, Jen. If you'd just rip your clothes off for a guy like that, how do I know that this means anything to you?"

His harsh words make me tear up a little bit, I have to admit. "It does!"

"I thought you would be different, Jen. Because of your..." he trails off as a stunned look overtakes his face. "Your..."

"My what?"

"Well, because you wear..."

"Hearing aids?" I yell it in his face, and he looks taken aback at my sudden rage. "You thought I'd be easy for you to keep because I wear hearing aids? Is that why you picked me out that day in the gym? Because I'd be easy for someone like you to attract and keep your eyes on?"

"No, no. Come on," he stammers, raising his hands in defense. "That's not what I meant at all."

"Okay, so what did you mean?" I put my hands on my hips, my most intimidating posture.

"I came over to meet you because I was impressed. I thought it was... interesting." He lets the word settle, catches my look of disapproval and tries again. "Not interesting... but, really brave."

"Brave? I need them to hear, Noah. They're not optional. It's not like I get up in the morning and think to myself, 'Oh man, what should I wear today with this adorable turtleneck sweater? I know! I'll put my hearing aids in so everyone thinks I'm freaking BRAVE.'"

"Come on, Jen. They brought me over to you and now we have…"

"What do we have, in your professional estimation? Huh? A really awesome time? A super-strong physical connection? A passion like you've felt with no other woman?" I wave him away from me and start to pull the door closed between us. "Whatever pointless, sexist line you're going to use on me, you can just forget it. I've already known too many guys like you."

Before the door closes, Noah puts his hand on it. I'm not strong enough to push it closed with him fighting me.

"Stop it," I rage, using the weight of my entire body on the door. "I want you to leave now."

"Not until you hear me out," he says, wrapping his fingers around the edge of the door and pushing it open far enough for us to clearly see each other. "Sometimes I don't say things as cleverly as you do, and sometimes the words come out wrong, even though I know what I'm trying to say. I came over to meet you that day because I admired you. I saw you working hard and keeping up with your sister, fighting both a physical disability and an obvious difference in your fitness levels. I wanted to meet you, because you seemed strong and determined. I liked that."

I stare him down for a moment, considering his words. Noah wasn't attracted to me that day, something I probably knew all along. But to hear him say it, and to discover that the one thing he was attracted to was the only thing about myself that I can never, ever change no matter how hard I try—it's all too much for me to process.

"I'd like you to leave now, Noah," I say quietly. I know I won't have to push on the door anymore, so I drop my hands down to my sides. "I don't want to be with someone who only sees me like that."

He scoffs at first, but when I raise my eyes to him and he sees the quiet anger and pain behind them, he stops trying.

"Fine," he says, throwing up his hands. "If that's the way you want this to end."

I swallow hard. "I'm not my hearing aids, Noah. I'm not some pet project you can rehabilitate and turn into whatever you want her to be. I have to be myself."

"That's all I ever wanted you to be. Don't you get it?"

I can't look at him, so I push the door closed, ending our conversation with the firm click of the lock. And then I stand there, letting the door support my back while I weep quiet tears. I don't know how long Noah stands outside, or if he can even hear me crying, but I can't really move from the door mat anyway. So I cry it out, until I sink down onto the floor in a heaping mess of running makeup, stringy hair, and damp clothing.

Look at that… it's raining after all.

CHAPTER TWENTY-TWO

Without the regular trips back and forth to Tom's Workout World, I'm a teeny bit afraid to even make eye contact with a scale. Which I know was ridiculous. Scales don't have eyes, Jen. But you know what I mean. A few packages of Oreos and a couple of weeks of missed gym trips is not exactly the right formula for substantial weight loss.

In fact, as I learn this morning, it had quite the opposite effect.

"Five frickin' pounds," I tell Lyla over coffee later that day. "I am a total disaster right now. What the hell am I supposed to do?"

"Buy a treadmill?" She suggests, playing with the plastic tab on her Dunkin Donuts lid.

"Will we have room for that in the apartment?" I think for a moment. "Maybe if we don't have a couch. That way, we have to work out when we watch TV."

"You know damn well that we'll just sit on the treadmill while we watch TV and eat a pint of ice cream, Jen."

The girl has a point. And she knows me better than I thought she did.

"All right, so now what?"

"Back to the gym?"

"I don't know if that's such a good idea. I can't face Noah... not yet. Maybe not ever." I shake my head, then pulled my hair back into a pony tail against the brisk wind of the spring day. I was tired of pulling pieces of it out of my mouth, after all. This is why Boston girls always have a hair elastic around their wrist when they spend any time outdoors.

"Have you talked to him at all? Was there any follow up whatsoever?"

I shook my head again, as I considered the dregs of my cold coffee. "It's going to be really awkward. I have enough of that in my life. I mean, we both said some unpleasant things."

"Are you actually listening to yourself talk right now? You're ridiculous."

"Why?"

"Because you had a fight. You're not the first couple in the universe to have a screaming match, then kiss and make up."

"I don't know if I want that," I say, twisting my hair around my finger. "I don't want to be with someone because of my hearing loss... I can't let that define me."

"Jen, I'm going to let you in on a little secret," Lyla leans in, covering her mouth with one hand. I expect her to whisper, but instead she speaks at full volume, sending me reeling backwards. "Everyone has something that defines them!"

Blinking, I stare at her for a moment. I have to adjust both of my hearing aids to stop the buzzing feedback before she can continue talking though.

"Look at that guy over there," she says, pointing to an overweight man sitting alone at a table. "He's letting his weight define him. Her, the blonde one there, gabbing away on her cell phone at full volume? She's letting that blonde hair define her as a bimbo stereotype. Just listen to what she's saying, for crying out loud. And me..."

"Cold-hearted psychoanalyst?" I take a guess.

"Close, but no," she says, grinning. "I let my sarcasm define me, my friend. But underneath that sarcasm, who am I?"

I sigh deeply, dropping my head into my hands.

"I'm a lot more than that, aren't I?" she continues. "Just like he's more than his weight, and she's more than a blonde. Well, maybe. But my point remains... you are more than your hearing aids, but that might be what defines you for some people. Deal with it, Jen. It could be a lot worse."

"I'd buy that card," I tease. "I can see it now: 'Smile! It could be worse!' Seriously, where do you get your advice?"

"Confucius, mostly." Lyla shrugs then takes a sip of her coffee. "Honestly, Jen, friend to friend... I don't think Noah defines you as the 'hearing loss' girl. That kind of fascination has an expiration date, you know? And his... well, he sounds like he's in it for the long haul."

Lyla's words stick with me into the night, interrupting my sleep, and well into the next morning. I understand what she means, but I just don't know how to process it all. And who was I kidding, thinking I could belong with Noah anyway? I'd be the mousy, overweight girlfriend who was always suspicious when he was out late, jealous of every girl he worked with and every client he took on. I couldn't live my life like that, not when I knew damn well how little self-esteem I already possessed.

What a mess I'd made.

When the day of the move finally arrives, I find myself experiencing some regrets... but all for a different reason. In retrospect, keeping that small army of tall, strapping men around long enough to help me move out of my parents' in-law apartment might have been a smart move on my part. But, as things stand, not a single one of them is interested in seeing me at all, so I'm on my own. Lyla came to help with her friend Ruby, but considering I can probably bench-press either one of them, my hopes aren't high for their ability to move a couch.

Why the hell didn't I just hire movers?

Fortunately, my dad is a superhero and has the afternoon free. As he spots Lyla and I struggling to move my dresser across the front lawn and into the moving van, he pops his head out the front door and asks if I want help. I stop, nearly dropping the furniture right onto the grass, and yell back a "Pleeeeease" to him. Lyla means well, but it just isn't happening for her.

Once we have the dresser in the truck, Dad commits himself to seeing my moving efforts through to the end. He takes apart my bed and moves the pieces on his own, hauls all the dresser drawers out one by one, and even carries the flat screen TV out for me. I occupy the two useless girls with a series of small items, like clothes on hangers, bags full of sheets and towels, or small boxes of DVDs and paperbacks. I carry the moderately heavy stuff out on my own, practically running circles around the skinny chicks.

It feels pretty good to be the fittest girl in my immediate vicinity for a change.

"Thanks, Dad," I say, dusting my hands off. He swings the door to the van shut and gives me a hug.

"Is there anything else I can do?"

"Lend me your drill?" I say, grinning. "So I can reassemble my bed?"

"You're sure you don't want me to come along?"

I shake my head. "I got it, Dad. You've already done more than enough."

I hug him again, and a wave of sorrow washes over me. I've left home before—to go to college out of town and into my own place while I was working. But this time, which I knew would be the last time, it's almost bittersweet. Having parents around all the time has been inconvenient most days, but when they aren't going to be just on the other side of the door, that makes me nervous.

Maybe my mom was right after all.

"Thanks again, Dad," I say, forcing a smile. "I'll be home for dinner on Sunday."

Because it's all about baby steps.

Dad watches us pull out of the driveway, careful not to critique the way I drive the van, and I wave to him as we drive off. One town over isn't too far away, after all. I'm going to be okay.

In my new apartment, with everything finally unpacked and settled in, I take some small comfort in having a roommate for the first time in several years. Although Lyla is a couple of years younger than me, we get along really well as co-habitants. She has similar neat-freak tendencies to mine, so there are never dishes piled up in the sink or rings around the inside of the toilet. Chores are mindless occupations we engage in simultaneously as a de-stressing technique. As weird as that sounds, it's the truth. Vacuuming, folding laundry, unloading the dishwasher… these are the perfect times of day to get some thinking done.

And during those times, and the quiet time we have every night while we each work on our research projects, I put the finishing touches on that paper. When Lyla finishes hers—a sociological study on the effects of modern media on the human psyche—we trade and read them through. I haven't spared a single thought, idea, or bit of personal information. My paper details the painful process of separating myself from the internet identity, what I figure to be an exaggerated example of how we all have to be two different people in today's world.

When Lyla finishes reading it, she doesn't have much to say about it.

"Holy shit," she eloquently comments. "I had no idea all this was going on. Some of it, sure… but wow!"

"Well, now you know why I was so desperate to get out on my own," I shrug.

"Yeah," she says, flipping through the pages again. "Holy shit indeed."

I make a few edits here and there, catch a couple of typographical errors, and then when I'm ready, I march it straight into Dr. Chase's office.

She smiles when she sees me. "I've missed having you in class this semester," she laughs. "Not as many scathing comments from these students."

"Yeah, that's my fault," I laugh back.

"How's this semester been for you?"

"It's done now," I say, handing her the portfolio containing my paper. "But let's say it's been a little more dramatic than I wanted it to be."

She flips through the pages, skimming a few lines as she goes along. Her eyes widen somewhere near the middle and she looks up at me.

"Thought you might like to read the unabridged version," I say. "But there's a formal one in there too. The version I'm officially submitting and would consider sending away for publication. I hope you don't mind. I only expect the grade for the formal version."

Or, the less boring version, as Lyla had put it.

"I'll read them both and just grade the formal one. But you never know, Jen," she closes the folder around my two papers. "Sometimes the scientific magazines like the juicy stuff."

To celebrate my completion of the program, finally, I go for a run. A legitimate, all-out, special-running-clothes run across Boston Common. And as I run, I suck in my stomach and keep my back straight to work my oblique muscles, just like Noah taught me. I focus on keeping my breath even, keeping the volume on my iPod low so I can hear passing bikers and other pedestrians. Yes, iPod headphones do work if you have hearing loss, you just have to crank it up a little.

And to be honest, as I'm running, I hope Noah will pop out from behind a bush somewhere and coach me along. I try to picture him running up ahead of me, taunting me to keep up with him and his perfectly fit physique. But as soon as I start to lose myself in the run, I lose the mental image as well. Eventually, I stop trying all together and just push myself forward.

Faster and faster and faster. I speed across the Common, lost in the rush of adrenaline and endorphins, without realizing how far I can push myself without a trainer at all. When I make it to the other end, I stop, bewildered and amazed at how quickly the time and distance has passed beneath the soles of my shoes.

All by myself, I have done this. Jennifer Smith is a runner and no one has to scream at her to make her do it. I let myself wind down, walking a quick loop around one of the many sitting areas on the Common, and then push myself forward again. I even take a longer detour through the Public Garden before I head for home.

Look at me go.

CHAPTER TWENTY-THREE

That night, I can feel myself getting irritable with boredom. With all my ties with friends and loved ones cut or fraying, and no sociology project to drown myself in (or Hostess cupcakes for that matter), I need to do something or I'll go insane.

In a bold move, I get up off the couch and walk straight into Lyla's room to see what she's up to for the night. It's risky, since Lyla is a more social and outgoing person than I am, but I need to do something that's not related to any men, sisters, or fake personas just for one night. After all, she keeps saying we should hang out sometime. Couldn't hurt to ask, could it?

"Yeah, let's do something," she says, as cheery as I've always known her to be. "A couple of us we're heading out for drinks downtown. Want to come along?"

It's enough of an incentive for me to put on something sexy from the back of my closet, spend ten minutes detailing the perfect smoky-eyed makeup look—complete with mascara—and even blow out my hair. I don't exactly look like a hooker when I'm done, but I look like I want to feel. Sexy and daring, flirty and vivacious. This is the way I've always felt inside, but I'd been hiding it with extra weight and baggy sweaters.

Not anymore. Jennifer Smith will be turning heads tonight, folks.

And I do, which is just so totally shocking to me, I can't figure out how to handle it. Lyla and her friends, a couple of girls from other BU graduate programs, are dressed similarly to myself, which does much to help me feel like I fit in. They're all single, all ready to dance, and all have an equally low tolerance for hard liquor. I keep my distance from the bar counter, mostly because it's crawling with sleazy men, and sip my one gin and tonic just for something to do.

When you're in a club, I quickly learn, it doesn't really matter where you're standing, the creeps will find you. Even minding my own business at a table toward the back of the room, they keep tracking me down. As Lyla and the other girls go off looking for guys—on purpose—I'm left to watch the purses and assorted feather boas, but only too happy to oblige.

In the ten to fifteen minutes I'm left alone, no less than six different guys come a-courting, so to speak. I'm pretty sure that there aren't any signs posted nearby me advertising free single women looking for a good time. Still, just to be sure, I turn around and check. Nope. They're just wandering over here on their own, armed with their best pick-up lines, and trying their hardest. Mostly, I just can't believe that any of these lines ever work on any woman.

That is, until I see Lyla's friend Ruby wander off with one of my rejects into a darkened corner of the club. Will wonders never cease?

It doesn't take long for me to tire of the electric, hormone-charged, alcohol-fueled atmosphere of the club scene. I know I don't belong here, but it has been nice to pretend for a change. Yes, I still feel like a sexy, outgoing Jennifer, but hanging out here is totally an Olivia thing to do. It's not my scene and these aren't really my friends. It's all an act. It's not any closer to being true to myself than playing Olivia online was.

What the heck am I doing here?

Even though my mother taught me never to go anywhere by myself, I ditch the club and everyone in it. I shoot Lyla an apologetic text message about not feeling well and just start walking down the street. I don't exactly have a destination in mind, I just know that I don't want to be in there anymore. It's not me, not Jennifer. And it's not the kind of person I want to be either.

That club was too much Olivia for me to handle.

Halfway between my new apartment and Tom's Workout World, I stop. I'm not really sure if I realized where I was heading and then stopped, or stopped first and realized it later. Should I just go home and call it a night? I could just leave it up to tomorrow to be a better day, pulling me from my poor excuse for a pity party. Or is it better to take a risk on Team Jennifer for a change?

I know what Olivia and Claire would do. I know what Sean would want me to do. I even know what my mother would advise. The one person I can't predict is the one person I want to find. I know what I have to do and in order to do it, these stupid giant heels need to go. Totally impractical for a late-night stroll.

So I take them off and toss them into my gigantic bag. I'm lucky big bags were in fashion this season, or I would've been stuck carrying them. Or worse, donating them to the nearest homeless person. I consider myself a charitable person, but not with a pair Manolo Blahniks inherited from my estranged sister. There's sentimental value there. Besides, what's a homeless person going to do with these strappy nightmares?

I'm not stingy, okay?

Anyway, shoes in my purse, I start walking. And walking and walking, and eventually, I stop walking and start jogging. Despite the five pounds and the back-slide I've started to my previous, less fit self, I can keep up a strong pace with little issue. So I keep going, careful to dodge broken glass and big rocks in my bare feet and trying not to think about how much gravel hurts to run on. Damn the pedicurist and her expert callous-filing techniques. If only I had a little bit of roughness on my soles, I might be okay.

Jogging along, it doesn't take long at all for me to find myself in the parking lot of Tom's Workout World. Noah's car is there, as I knew it would be, facing the front doors of the gym. Heaving for air, I lean back onto his hood to give myself a moment. I rub my sore feet until the throbbing subsides and then slip on my gorgeous shoes once again.

I wince for the first few steps, remind myself that beauty is pain, and march forward with determination in my gaze. I don't need to waste any more time goofing around. I know who Jennifer Smith is now and I know what she wants.

And if he doesn't want me back, well... I'll deal with it in due time.

Instead of dwelling on the "what ifs" as I might have done before, I decide not to think about it, concentrating my energy on making only one possibility a reality. Still, facing him is harder than I expect. When I push through the front door and find him packing up for the night, I almost lose all my resolve and run away.

"Jen," he says, startled. "What are you..."

"Hi," I interrupt him, my nerves jolting me forward through the door. I try not to fidget with my skirt too much or trip on my own feet as I cross the gym floor. Dressed like this, I'm sure I look pretty ridiculous in a gym after hours.

"You look great." He states it simply, so it's hard to read anything more or less than a comment on the truth. 'You've been keeping up with your workouts?"

I nod, embarrassed to admit to finding success on my own. I don't know why that embarrasses me. Maybe I just feel guilty for taking our special connection and destroying it with my own self-reliance. Which is completely ridiculous.

"That's great," he says, his mouth forming the slightest smile. "I'm really proud of you. I always said you didn't need me."

I wince, stung by his comment.

"I didn't mean it that way," he says immediately, wincing himself. "I just meant that you always had it in you and you didn't need me playing the motivator, barking orders at you all the time."

"I know," I mutter, careful to look away instead of betraying my relief. He can read me like a book no matter what I do, but I have to try at the very least. "But I did like having you around. It was nice to have a run buddy, you know?"

"Well, I'm just closing up," says Noah, master of the obvious. He adjusts the strap of the bag higher up onto his shoulder, hitting the switch on his way by. A single row of recessed lights illuminates the front of the gym now, sending a cascade of glittering light out from my sequined top. Like I'm a giant disco ball or something. He walks toward me, making his pathetic small talk all the way but I'm interested. "So, I guess, I'll see you later? Are you going to start coming back to the gym now or have you been going somewhere else?"

I don't want to let this charade go on anymore. There's too much here that needs to be said, and I'm going to start saying it.

"Can we talk?" I say boldly, stepping in front of him.

His mouth forms a tight line as he considers me.

"Please, Noah. I have... Some things I'd like to say."

Wordlessly, he sits down on the nearest bench and waits for me to speak. After the horrible things I've said to him, I know I'm lucky just to get his attention. And then, once I realize the magnitude of powerful stare on me, I can't remember what I meant to say anyhow. He looks at his watch, just obviously enough to make me nervous, so I stutter right into my opening line.

"Everything that's been going on in my life, these past months... This whole semester, really. I mean, Sean and Olivia, Claire, the project, the fighting... Everything," I pause, and his eyes lift to meet mine. "It was all fake. All a game. I let it take over me and it did things to who I was. I—"

"Don't try to make excuses, Jen," he warns, though gently. "You said that stuff, not Olivia."

"I know," I say, a bit defensively. "I'm getting to that, okay? I did say those things and for that, I'm truly sorry. I just wanted you to know that, in all this time, I should've appreciated the one thing in my life that was truly real."

He blinks at me for a moment, saying nothing.

"You, Noah. None of that other stuff was real at all, but you always were. You might've had your reasons for meeting me, but

I'm lucky that you did. Because of that, we found something together. And even though I didn't see it at the time, I do now. I'm sorry."

I give it a moment, letting the words echo in the empty gym around us. But eventually, I just can't stand the silence anymore. I need to hear something from him, anything, even if it's not positive. Finally, I look over to him and find a thoughtful gaze, but nothing behind those eyes that I can interpret as good. I decide to save my dignity then and I walk out, not daring to look behind me.

I just turn on those spiky heels and walk my little butt right out of that awkward situation.

Outside and alone, I really regret not taking a cab down here, not because I'm too tired to walk home but because my feet are ready to stage an anarchy at any moment. Conscious that Noah might still be watching me as I toddle my way across the parking lot, I leave the shoes on my aching feet, forcing myself to practice Claire's walk all the way out of his line of sight.

In my head, I'm singing a chorus of ouches with every single step, and still I roll slowly from my heel to my toe, heel to toe, heel to toe. Sashaying, swaying, each step deliberate.

If I were Claire, I'd instead be counting down in my head to the moment I hear Noah call out my name and tell me to stop. But I'm Jennifer, and although I have newfound self-esteem, I'm not about to start acting like I keep men on a leash behind me. Noah can do what's right for Noah, what he feels in his heart. I've said my piece and now I just have to wait for him to make up his mind.

He'll find me when he knows what he wants… provided I'm even what he wants.

Somewhere around my twenty-fifth step away from Tom's Workout World, I hear the door clang shut. That door doesn't normally make any noise when it shuts, unless someone pushes it closed, wanting me to hear it. I turn and there he is, his hands on his hips.

"I promised you I'd make you hear every word," he says, practically yelling. "And I'll make you hear every noise too, if that's what it takes."

With two car lengths between us, I want to run to him. Two things hold me back: my dignity and these stupid, stupid shoes. Instead, I take my well-practiced steps back in his direction. He walks out to meet me halfway.

"Noah—" I say, out of breath with anticipation.

"No, it's my turn now," he says, in a more commanding tone than I've ever heard him use on the gym floor with a stubborn client. It commands attention. It's totally sexy. "Of course it was wrong of me to approach you for the reasons I did. You're not someone to be stared at and mocked, as you seem to think. Whatever happened to you in school, with other kids, none of that matters anymore, Jen. You're a beautiful woman, smart and funny, with a slight disadvantage that you have more than overcome. It shouldn't matter to you what got my attention in the first place, not when I feel the way I do about you now."

I sniffle, wiping a rogue tear from my cheek. I don't want to cry, so I bite down on my tongue and look him straight in the eye.

"I love you, Jen." He brushes the back of his hand along my cheek. "And I don't love you because of or despite one stupid detail. I love you just as you are."

When he leans down to kiss me, the pain in my feet suddenly vanishes. My stomach does a back-flip inside my tensed body. I don't know what to say or do, aside from letting him continue to kiss me. His gentle lips release mine, kiss me sweetly once more, and then move away from me.

"I've been such an idiot," I sigh, wrapping my arms around his neck.

"Nah," he laughs lightly. "You're just too thick-skulled for your own good."

"Have you been talking to my mother?" I chuckle.

"Nice shoes, by the way," he says, craning his neck around to see them. "Nice and high."

"You like that?"

"It means I could do this more easily." He kisses me again, more deeply this time. I decide that I too prefer the added height and shall invest in a small army of such shoes just for occasions like this. His slow kiss grows more passionate, turning into a fury of short kisses up and down my neck. His hot lips send a chill across my skin, lighting that fire all over again. Like we haven't missed a step at all.

Noah's hands press me against him and I respond to his every touch, thrilled beyond words. As he starts to pull me towards his car, the only one in the emptied parking lot, I catch the glint in his eye. The naughty teenager out on a date, scouting out the perfect spot for a "parking" encounter. I let him lead me there, just as turned on by the idea as he seems to be, but then something stops me just as he opens the back door to his sedan.

"Wait," I say, pushing away from him. "I didn't... I have to..."

He raises an eyebrow.

"I love you, too," I grin up at him.

Noah's answering smile quickly becomes another round of kisses and, eventually, we find our way into that back seat after all.

EPILOGUE

My name is Jennifer Smith, but my friends and family just call me Jen. You can friend me on Facebook, follow me on Twitter, or read my blog *Confessions of an Alter-Ego*, but you won't be able to learn all there is to know about me there. Not unless you spend the time to get to know me in person.

See, online, you'd never know that I have a Master's degree in Sociology with a focus on modern communication, or that I'd spent the better part of a year being two people at the same time. Or that I'd recently been two points in a complicated love square. That's right: *two* points.

And while my relationship status on Facebook might reveal that I am "in a relationship" with Noah Wayland, it won't tell you how totally and completely in love we are. Or that we're planning to secretly elope next month to the Bahamas with just our closest loved ones. Facebook doesn't even know about it… because then it wouldn't be very secret at all, would it?

It *will* tell you that I have a sister named Claire, but not how much we mean to each other. I'm not sure that I can even put that into words, come to think of it. But after a brief time of not speaking to each other, I'm happy to report that Claire will be serving as my maid of honor next month. And she'll also be bringing along a very special guy as her date—a man named

David whom she met through an online dating service and who fell in love with her before ever laying eyes on her. Give them a little time, and they'll be walking down the aisle themselves before you know it.

Facebook also can't tell you how much I've learned about myself and humanity in general, thanks to this little experiment. People like Olivia, Tom, and Sean really do exist. They're out there. And when you do meet them, you may think they're as cool and as perfect as any people can be. The truth is, you never know who they *really* are inside, not when they're putting on such a good show. And if you let yourself get swept away by one of them (or by something like a soul-crushing sociological experiment), you're only hurting yourself in the end.

So yeah… I might have the world's plainest, most boring name. I might not be scorching hot like my sister. I might have to wear hearing aids just to function like "normal" people. And I might not exactly have lost that last ten pounds… yet.

But I know who I am and I love that person. I wouldn't trade being Jennifer for anything in the world.

ABOUT THE AUTHOR

Stephanie Haddad is a full-time mom by day and a writer by naptime. She lives in the Boston area with her loving husband, precocious toddler, and cuddly dog. While her short fiction has appeared in several online publications and won a handful of contests, her novel publishing career only began in 2011. She is also the author of *A Previous Engagement*, *Love Regifted* and *Love Unlisted*. Visit her website www.stephaniehaddad.com for more information on forthcoming titles.

Made in the USA
San Bernardino, CA
23 April 2016